I0601023

WHITEOUT

UNEXPECTED BOOK ONE

ANN GRECH

ISBN: 978-0-9954321-3-0

Ann Grech may be contacted via the following email address:

ann@anngrech.com

BLURB

The closeted sports star and a straight paramedic, the heli-skiing trip that traps the two men on a mountain and a game of twenty questions. What could go wrong? Or will it be the moment they get all they've ever wanted? In discovering their bisexuality, will Reef and Ford be brave enough to reach for each other?

Pro-snowboarder, Reef Reid, is at the peak of his career. He has it all. Except the one thing he desperately wants: a lover, the white picket fence and his happily ever after. Disillusioned and exhausted, he flees to a tropical paradise to defrost.

But a ticketing mishap lands him in the ski village of Queenstown, New Zealand.

Stratford 'Ford' Wallace loves the ladies, but rarely sticks around longer than a night. Falling for a man wasn't on the cards, but everything he knows is flipped on its head when the enigmatic Reef Reid literally drops out of the sky.

When a whiteout traps them on a mountaintop neither expects sparks to ignite. They're unable to resist each other, but will they give into temptation? Or will the avalanche that tears through the mountain end them?

Whiteout is book one in Ann Grech's international hit male/male romance series, Unexpected. Books 2 and 3 continue Reef and Ford's story through the highs and lows of the pro-snowboarding circuit. You'll fall in love, want to slap a certain someone or two and swoon over these two men who are made for each other.

DEDICATION

For M, B and J.
Always for you.

ACKNOWLEDGMENTS

My biggest thank you goes to my hubby and kids for putting up with their pre-occupied wife/mum. Late dinners, a messy house and me stressing about ridiculous, self-imposed deadlines never faze you. You have no idea how grateful I am for you all being so willing to put up with my crap! Your unwavering encouragement and support means the world to me. I love you more than words can express.

I'm lucky enough to have put this story together with the help of a fantastic bunch of friends. Thank you to all of you: my amazing crit-partner, Kariss Stone - love ya lady xx, my cover designer Willsin Rowe (whose design, once again, exceeded my dreams a hundredfold), my editors Sassie Lewis and Susan Child for critiquing and editing your asses off and for dropping everything to help me out – you are both wonderful – and to my beautiful friend and lifesaver, Maci Dillon. Without you, I would have gone insane by now. Thank you for your support lovely lady xx

To the bloggers and readers who have reviewed my other books and who have reviewed this one too, without you I wouldn't have had the success I've had so far. Your support and selfless help is amazing and so very appreciated. Thank you.

This story couldn't have been written without inspiration from my favorite MM authors. There are too many to name here, too many characters to list, too many book boyfriends to cheer on when they get their happy endings, but it's you who motivates me go back and buy every book in your collection, who gives me the idea for a fantastic story at 2am (okay, the 2am thing might be me!) and you who I want to be like when I grow up ;-)

And finally, to my readers. I may get inspiration from the people I meet and places I go and the stories I read, but you motivate me. Thank you for pushing me to do better.

Hope you all fall in love with Reef and Ford too.

Ann xx

CHAPTER ONE

REEF LEANED his head back and attempted, albeit unsuccessfully, to stretch his long legs out. He was used to flying, used to the cramped seating but it never got any easier. And he wasn't even supposed to be on this flight. Momma Bear, his mom – for all intents and purposes – except by blood, still insisted on booking his trips. She'd thought he wanted Queens*town*, New Zealand. He'd actually wanted Queens*land*, Australia. He hadn't even realized the mistake until arriving at the airport to check-in, but by then he couldn't change his flight. As a pro-snowboarder, he'd been chasing winter for nearly fifteen years. All he wanted to do was to lie on a beach and get a tan, to feel the warmth of the hot sun on his skin. Defrost. Rest. Try and figure out why things had turned so bad with Addilyn.

For the first time in over two years, he was single and could kick back and chill; enjoy himself for a bit. Sure, white sand, palm trees and surf would have been perfect for that, but hell, he wasn't going to mope around. Queenstown – another ski resort – wasn't exactly where Reef had planned on being during his season off, but he was going to take his sponsor's advice – relax and get his mojo back. Reef was actually looking forward to his impromptu trip to New Zealand. In the few hours he'd waited to board the plane he'd done some research. And damn, it looked fun.

As the plane taxied to a halt in front of the arrivals terminal in the small airport, Reef stretched his neck again and looked out the portal window. He'd seen countless mountains before but he was mesmerized by the view. Green hills surrounded them, with an absolutely spectacular mountain range only a short distance away. He could clearly see the chairlift going up the manicured white slopes of a nearby resort, its peak glittering in the brilliant sunshine.

Reef smiled and winked at the flight attendant as he dismounted the stairs and crossed the tarmac toward the terminal. Dialing Momma Bear's number as he entered the baggage claim, he smiled wider as he heard her sleepy voice answer after barely a ring. "Reef, you made it okay?"

"Yeah, I did. Sorry I woke you. What time is it there?" He stepped to the side, avoiding the stream of people making their way through the terminal. Noise surrounded him, but it was quiet on the other end of the line.

"Two in the morning." *That explains the quiet.*

"I wish you'd let me wait to call you at a more decent time."

"Honey, I've been up waiting for your call. Now I know you're safe, I can sleep properly. If you waited, I'd just be up for longer. It's better this way." A crying baby, a screaming toddler and two frustrated parents attempting to end the little boy's monster temper tantrum a few feet away from him prompted Reef to start walking again, pressing his finger against his other ear to block out the hum of excited chatter.

"I'll let you go and sleep then. Tell Coach I said hi."

"Just a second, honey. Addilyn called again. You aren't thinking about getting back together with her, are you?" He stopped dead in his tracks, the person behind Reef walking straight into him, muttering abuse at him for stopping.

"Hell no." Grinding his teeth, he fought down the wave of anger at the girl he thought he'd end up marrying. Reef unclenched his fist and ran his free hand through his dirty blonde hair to tug on the ends, making it stand up every which way. Getting angry at Addilyn again wouldn't help him, especially while he was speaking to Momma Bear.

"If she really loved me, she wouldn't have cheated. I'm not going to take her back. I can't trust her." The one thing Reef couldn't stand was cheating and Addilyn had confessed through tear-filled eyes to having repeated affairs with more than one of her photographers. Reef knew he was anything but perfect, but on the endless months that he and Addilyn had spent apart over the last couple of years, he never strayed. It pissed him off that she had.

"Okay, honey. Good, I'm glad to hear that. You know I never liked her anyway. She was never good enough for you."

"Momma Bear, only you would say that a catwalk model wasn't good enough for me."

"Model schmodel. It's what's in her heart that matters, and hers only sees dollar signs. We spoke for nearly fifteen minutes and eleven of those she talked about her career. She barely mentioned you and she was calling me so I'd persuade you to take her back."

"What did you say to her?"

"I told her that you have standards and they are well above her. I might have mentioned that you were going on vacation to spend the summer with a new flame too."

Chuckling, Reef shook his head. "You always know what to say, Momma Bear."

"She wasn't happy. And you know, it wouldn't kill you to get out there and have some fun. Be single for a while, enjoy life. Sow your wild oats. But don't forget to wrap it."

"Stop, stop." Reef cringed. "Coach gave me the talk when I was a kid. That was bad enough. Please don't make me go through it again."

The older woman let out a booming laugh into the phone. "I've emailed you a list of flights and accommodation options for a couple of the Barrier Reef islands so you can leave in the next day or two. Let me know what you'd prefer and I'll book them first thing tomorrow."

"Don't rush, it's gorgeous here. I wouldn't mind having a look, stick around for a bit."

"Okay, honey. You just let me know. Love you."

"You too, Momma Bear."

The auburn-haired girl standing next to Reef grinned at him. She was stunning. Barely clearing his shoulder, she rocked a set of damn sexy curves. She looked like a naughty version of that Disney mermaid. Dressed in tight faded blue jeans and a white tank top, with a bulky woolen cardigan slung over her arm, she smirked as he let his eyes travel down the length of her. The fur boots she wore had him laughing out loud. Bright purple. She was cute and feisty. He liked that.

"Momma Bear?" she drawled in a strong southern accent.

"Yeah, she always makes me call her as soon as I land."

"Your momma sounds sweet."

"Nah, she's not my mom. She and Coach kinda adopted me."

"Oh, I'm sorry, I didn't... I'm sorry about your parents."

Laughing, Reef shook his head. "Nah, Petal and River – my parents – are alive and well. Momma Bear isn't my actual adopted mom, but she might as well be."

"Oh, okay." She smiled and stuck out her hand. "I'm Cassie, Cassie Lane."

"Reef Reid. Nice to meet you."

"Where ya from, Reef?"

"Vermont originally, but I travel a lot so my accent has changed a bit. You?"

"Lil' town outside of Phoenix, but I'm based in Florida now." As an expensive grey suitcase approached them on the baggage carousel, she motioned toward it. "That's me. Enjoy your vacation, Reef."

"You too." He grinned as he lifted the bag off and handed it to her as another man approached them, wrapped his arm around Cassie and lifted the handle on the case. *Typical, all the cute ones are taken.* Probably for the best anyway – he did *not* want a repeat of all the shit that went down with Addilyn.

Constantly travelling, Reef lived out of a suitcase. He'd learned the hard way that he could comfortably manage a backpack, suitcase and board bag. Anything more than that was too damn hard to carry. Reef waited patiently as his bags emerged and followed the throng of people through customs then to the arrivals lounge.

Momma Bear organized a driver to take him to the hotel she booked. Those extra little things – in addition to everything else – made Reef love the woman even more than he already did. Having support in managing his competition and travel schedule, visas, promo event appearances and endorsements was a huge help. It meant that Reef could focus on practicing and competing, pushing himself to new heights and mastering harder tricks with every new season.

The ride in the back of the SUV to the hotel was short. From the quick glances he got travelling down the main street, it looked like a rockin' resort town. Tired, but elated looking skiers coming off the mountain carrying all their gear dodged the people spilling onto the sidewalks talking, and laughing near the bars and burger joints. Buskers played on a couple of the street corners drawing a crowd to them. Kids clowned around in the pocket parks on their skateboards and tourists ate ice creams and shopped at the high-end boutiques. And from the amount of clubs he saw signs for, the village would be even busier at night. Just the sort of town needed to get him out of this funk.

PUSHING through the door of his hotel suite, Reef let out a low whistle. Momma Bear had gone all out. It had one of the biggest wall-mounted TV's he'd ever seen. And the king sized bed? He could sink into it and not resurface for a week, but the jetlag would keep him up all night if he slept now. Nope, checking out the town was firmly on the agenda. It was a hella good excuse to get a beer if nothing else. And if the women here were anything like Cassie—even though she'd clearly been with the other dude—he'd be tempted to get back in the dating game.

He was ready in ten minutes; showered and dressed in a fresh pair of jeans, a comfy black V-necked long sleeved shirt, and black beanie. Food, beer and a band were top priority. Bungee jumping and jet boating were next up. Time to get the party started.

———

"OKAY MARK, I've got you. Lie back and relax while I get you down the mountain."

"C-c-c-cold."

"Yeah, we'll get you inside and warmed up. Hold tight, it's pretty steep here." Stratford Wallace, Ford to everyone who knew him, clicked his boots into his skis and towed the sled behind him as he started down the black diamond run, the steepest slope on the mountain. This was the best part of his job. Rescuing people was reward in itself, but being able to ski day in and day out, in conditions as perfect as they were at the moment, well that was priceless. The freedom of the cold wind whipping onto his face, the contrast of pure white against the bright blue sky, the crunch of the snow under his boots, the rush of skiing in fresh powder as Ford flew down the slopes turned his job into a passion.

The usual discussion – argument really – that he had with his father, was that he didn't want to be like the last three generations of Wallace men and become a surgeon. The thought of being stuck in the center of London that close to his parents? He would have ended up stressed to his eyeballs. Sure, he'd be loaded. He'd be living in an apartment during the week, and be able to unwind in his country estate on weekends. He preferred living in his modest cottage at the foot of the mountains. And every morning when he woke, he was filled with absolute joy at the prospect of heading to work. There was no chance he would have enjoyed working with his father. The man made him miserable.

Zigzagging down the slope to manage their speed, Ford got the terrified, almost catatonic and hypothermic Mark, to the safety of the rescue center at the mountain's base. If nothing else, the long run down the mountain gave him time to think about his plans for the night: hit up his favorite bar and head home with a cute snow bunny.

Shaking out of the daydream, Ford pulled up at the entry doors and hollered for Trent, the other paramedic stationed at The Remarkables, to help him. Both men lifted the injured skier from the stretcher onto a gurney, before wheeling him into the warm room and tugging off his boots. The stench of ammonia hit Ford as he peeled off Mark's soaking wet socks.

"S-s-sorry." Mark shivered again, despite Trent having removed his jacket and thermal shirt and replaced them with the warm blanket now slung around his shoulders.

"No issue, Mark."

"She left me there. I was stupid; trying to impress her, but I got fuckin' terrified." Mark shivered, stuttering his words.

"How do you know her?"

Shaking his head, more quakes rocked Mark as he answered, "I don't. Just met her today."

"Bitch," Trent uttered as he passed Mark a hot cocoa. "Drink this, bro. We need to warm you up."

"Thanks." Mark took a few sips and cupped the mug in both hands, holding the blanket tightly around his shoulders at the same time. Once his shaking had stopped, Mark continued. "I'm fuckin' embarrassed. Sorry you had to deal with that. I'll get the rest of my kit off and get cleaned up."

"Hey, buddy. It's okay." Trent answered. "You aren't the first and you won't be the last person who freaks out. The first time you go down a slope like that, it's damn scary. I nearly shit myself the first time I went down a black diamond run and I was an experienced skier. Skids in my boxers and all."

Rolling his eyes at Trent's blunt and colorful response, Ford added. "It's our job to look after you. Don't stress."

"And anyway, it's Ford cleanin' ya up, so we're all good."

"Shut up, dumbass." Ford laughed. "Drink up. We need to stabilize your body temperature again so we can get you off the mountain and have you admitted into hospital. I want you checked out to make sure you're okay."

Mark nodded then took another sip of his drink. "What part of England are you from?"

"Ascot, just outside of London," Ford replied. "You been there?"

"No, I want to though."

Moving to the cupboard to get a bag for Mark's wet clothes, the landline rang. Reaching for the phone, Ford placed it on his shoulder. "Mountain Rescue, this is Ford."

"Hi Ford, this is Shelly from Up-High Heli-ski."

"Hiya, beautiful lady. How are you today?"

"I'm well, Ford, you incorrigible flirt. You?"

"I'd be better if you agreed to that date I've been asking you on since I got back." Ford grinned. She always turned him down but he wasn't upset. Their banter kept him laughing.

"I'm a relationship kinda girl, Ford. As much as those blue eyes of yours suck me in, I'm not in the market for what you're offering."

"You wound me, Shelly."

She giggled. "Back to business. We've had a booking for an overnight back trail heli-tour. You sent me an email last week about being the guide for the next trip?"

"I did, beautiful, thanks for remembering. We need to get up there and re-check the avalanche zones."

"That'd be great. I'm sure the customer would appreciate the company, too."

"How good a skier is he?"

"Snowboarder, not skier and he said he's good enough to go unaccompanied. But you know our policy, we don't let anyone go alone."

"Yeah, crazy. But at least he can ski." Ford didn't want to babysit anyone, so having someone who was actually experienced, rather than someone who just thought they were, was a bonus. It'd mean that he could make sure that the less-skied trails outside the groomed and patrolled ski resorts were still safe after the recent big dumps of snow. As the senior paramedic, it was Ford who would be doing any rescues of heli-skiers. The last thing he wanted was to have an unstable slope during a rescue. Call him pedantic, but he liked checking the more commonly used back trails himself.

———

"OKAY, the drop point is just up ahead, gents. Strap in and get ready to rock and roll."

"Really, Ricky? You still using that line?" Ford asked, laughing.

"Ford, you're the only person who doesn't appreciate my humor. Everyone else knows I'm the eccentric pilot."

"Really, dude? You sound like you're tryin' too hard." The snowboarder, Reef, grinned wickedly, deep dimples showing in his cheeks, his warm brown eyes lighting up. Wait, warm brown eyes? Since when did he even notice shit like that?

Ricky's reaction to Reef's comment was comical, shooting him a cross between a glare and a pout over his shoulder. Sitting there looking at Reef, Ford knew he'd have good form. Tall and lean, he was clearly fit. His gear was well loved and he barely had to look at what he was doing, fastening the bindings to secure his boots to the board. Ford watched him and followed, clipping his own boots onto the skis and zipping his jacket the rest of the way up. Running his fingers through his hair, he pushed the too-long brown curls out of his eyes before tugging on his helmet and pulling his goggles down into place. Ski poles on his wrists, he shuffled to the open door of the helicopter and positioned himself to jump.

Keying the mic for the helmet-mounted radio, Ford tested the clarity of the connection. "Base, this is Ford. Can you hear me?"

"Hearing you loud and clear, Ford."

"Beautiful lady!" Ford's British accent sounded stronger through the radio.

"You boys be safe." Shelly giggled, changing the subject.

"Copy that, base."

"Okay, Ford, you first. Get ready to jump. I'll give the go-ahead in three. Two. One. Go."

Ford cleared the struts of the helicopter with ease, jumping the eight foot drop to the steep slope below him. Loose powder reached his thighs as he glided a few yards out of the immediate drop zone that Reef would momentarily be landing into.

If Reef was as good a snowboarder as he thought he'd be, Ford knew they'd have a blast. Today would be less work and more play. Glued to the sight of Reef jumping from the helicopter, he appreciated how the man held himself, how easily he moved. Ford's musing was cut short when Reef sprayed an arc of snow at him as he neared, flashing those dimples and a wicked smile again.

CHAPTER TWO

REEF ALREADY LIKED HIS GUIDE. The dude was laid back, but professional as hell. And smart. He'd insisted on looking at the weather maps himself, interpreting the likelihood of getting caught in the storm front that was just under a hundred miles away. Satisfied that the wind was tracking away from them, Ford had cleared the trip, only to insist on checking the provisions that were being dropped at the overnight camp site. Reef had watched him, enthralled.

Seeing the guy jump out of the helicopter made Reef's excitement ramp up as adrenaline coursed through his veins. Ford's form was perfection. Thick strong muscles controlled every movement he made and Reef could appreciate that he looked good doing it. It was the kind of perfection he strove to achieve in every competition. Ford's moves inspired him. Reef shook his head. He'd wanted to get away from the snow, but who was he kidding? Snowboarding, the rush, the excitement? It was in his blood. This was who Reef was. Snowboarding was everything to him.

"Reef, your turn. Three. Two. One. Go."

As Reef pushed out of the helicopter's cabin he braced himself for the impact, legs bent and arms out wide, his typical landing position. His board connected with the soft snow and he sunk down to his waist in loose powder that seemed to float around him. He'd been heli-skiing countless times in the U.S. and throughout Europe when he was on tour, and even in Southern America when he'd spent the northern summers training. But the thrill of that first landing never dulled. Pointing his snowboard down the slope he began to slide, skiing toward his guide who was watching his moves. Reef couldn't resist, turning at the last moment to spray Ford with the wake from his board. The other man smirked at him before taking off like a bullet, cutting in and out along the full width of the slope, sending up arcs of powder with every turn he made.

Cold air rushed past him as Reef shot down. The fresh snow swirling around his knees rustled, so unlike the crackling of the icy runs on most ski resorts' manicured trails. Rolling white clouds topped the range on one side of him, and on the other, the sun sat in a clear blue sky making the snow glitter the brightest of whites. This was freedom, the board that was an extension of himself, and the speed, made him feel whole. It was refreshing not having the pressure that came with competing and trying to execute the perfect jump. He thought he needed a break from the snow, but he was wrong. Reef didn't need the distance, just relief from the pressure of performing at world championship levels. Reef would never lose his love of snowboarding, how could he? He was in his element.

Reef's headset crackled before Ford's accented voice came through the speaker. "Nice landing, mate. In about five hundred feet, take the left hand side of the crevasse. The right side has a rocky cliff that you don't want to try jumping off."

Keying the mic, Reef answered, "Copy, dude. And thanks, you nailed your landing too."

Silence filled the air again as Reef closed his eyes and breathed deep, enjoying the burn of the cold air flowing into his lungs as he cut across to the right. Taking a wide arc, he bent and ran his gloved hand through the powdered snow, the flakes sliding between his fingers as he tracked them. Straightening his stance again he shot to the right, moving almost horizontally along the mountain. He could clearly see the ravine up ahead. Leaving plenty of space and time to move to the correct side of the slope, Reef leaned into the mountain, turning his board to the left and lining up with Ford's figure ahead of him.

Serious form. Reef watched Ford zigzagging like a pro on a set of skis. He made it look graceful, easy, effortless. Ford was one of those guys beginners would watch on YouTube and get inspired by; the sort of guy that Reef idolized as a kid. Not that Ford was old. There was only five, maybe six, years difference between them.

Ford pointed to the left with his ski pole when he neared the split in the slope and glanced over his shoulder. "Right behind you, Ford," Reef said into the radio.

"I need to stop up ahead and get some photos. There's an avalanche prone area along that ridge across from us and we've had a few big dumps recently. I might need to get someone up there to set off some charges to clear any threats. Slopes are pretty clear of hazards for the next hour or so of skiing but I'd prefer for us to stick together." The face across from them that Ford motioned to was a pristine white. Untouched snow as far as the eye could see was tempting, except for the ugly crack that tracked through its middle. Piled up snow overhung a black cliff at the top of the almost vertical slope. It screamed danger. And not in a good way.

"No worries. I'll stay close," Reef responded. Pointing up to the darkening sky, he asked, "Hey, do those clouds look like they're getting heavier?"

"Yeah, I've been watching them too. There's been a shift in the wind. I don't think it's the storm front but you never know out here. I'm gonna radio base when we stop. I'm getting static here."

"Aren't these radios designed to communicate over the mountains?"

"Yep. It's not great that I'm not getting through. I'm not overly concerned yet, but if I can't make contact further around the mountain, I might have to reconsider our plans."

"What, get the chopper back?" Reef questioned as he cut against the slope in another wide arc.

"Can't get it back unless we can get through. I'll change the trails I was planning to take you on to more sheltered ones. They aren't as challenging, but safer if the weather sets in." Pointing up to a cluster of rocks, Ford added. "Stop up at that outcrop."

Reef watched as Ford flicked his skis to face side-on to the slope and clicked out of them, planting them upright in the snow with his poles. Reef had watched many a beginner lose their skis or board from just lying them down. People often forgot that low friction surfaces and skis and boards designed to slide make for hilarious home videos, usually of parents running after their kids' wayward gear.

Keying the mic in his helmet, Ford hailed the base, but nothing except static came through. "Dammit, this isn't good. Base is on the other side of that mountain over there." Ford pointed at the summit immediately before them that had dark clouds roiling around its peak. "I've always been able to get through to them from here. And that weather is turning fast."

"Maybe it's your equipment. Lemmie try." Reef pressed the mic on his headset and called out, "Base this is Reef on the heli-tour. Do you copy?"

Static crackled through the line before a frantic, "Reef? Ford?... storm... changed... now."

Reef shot his wide-eyed gaze over to Ford. "Did you hear that?"

"Fuck. Yes."

"Repeat, base. Did not receive your message."

This time the words were clearer, but still filled with static. "Winds unexpectedly changed. Storm rapidly moving in. Blizzard conditions. Take shelter immediately."

"Copy base, we're on the move. Over." Ford had already snapped one foot into his ski and had the other lined up with his poles around his wrists. "If this blizzard lasts any longer than a few hours, the overnight camp isn't going to give us enough shelter. There's a ranger's hut in the next valley, but to get to it, we're gonna have to go through the pass. We'll have to walk part of it, and quickly."

"Can we make it?"

"I don't know, but we can't stay here."

"Let's go."

"Fast and hard, Reef. Stay close to me."

Reef nodded. He was used to doing his own thing and he may be at home in the mountains, but his competitions were usually held on clear days. After all, a competition was useless if neither the spectators, nor the judges, could see your moves. Even practice tended to be in good conditions so his coach could give him pointers, heavy snow days were for yoga and Pilates so he could maintain his balance and flexibility. It had been a while since he'd been hit with anything more than a mild dump while out in the wilds, certainly nothing heavy enough to close down a mountain like the one tracking toward them. This was no small storm, and Reef was not a survival expert like Ford. The fact was, he was freaking out about being so far into the backcountry, with the prospect of being hammered by a blizzard. Ford taking the lead was a relief; he respected him.

His guide didn't wait for Reef to say anything as he turned and cut along the slope. They were following the ridgeline, but barely dropping in elevation. Reef could see up ahead where the two mountains joined to form a valley that ran only a hundred feet, or so, higher than they currently were. Reef followed, a new kind of adrenaline pumping through his body. It was a little fear mixed with nerves – that excited energy he got right before the start of a competition. Except, suddenly, a lot more was at stake.

———

NOT GOOD. Not fucking good. Losing radio contact like that only meant one thing – one hell of a storm. What Ford didn't understand was how none of the forecasts had picked up the wind change. He'd checked, and double-checked them. Usually a front moving through like that was predictable well in advance. There was absolutely no indication of it coming anywhere near Queenstown or the range he was currently skiing on. Now, he had a potential life-threatening situation on his hands. The overnight camp was under a bluff out of the wind, but it wouldn't be protected from blizzard-like conditions. Snowfalls measuring anything over a foot would make a fire impossible, not to mention the wind. The camp would be like entering a deep freezer and sleeping in it. Even with their specially designed tents and sleeping bags and the thermal gear they were wearing, there was no way they'd be comfortable. Hell, surviving it would be a challenge.

So now, he found himself hoping against hope that the man flying along only twenty feet or so behind him was as competent a snowboarder as he had seemed to be so far. The fear that flashed over his brown eyes before determination set in didn't surprise Ford, but he was worried. His job was to keep people safe and he'd damn well do that. Although they hadn't spoken much, Ford already felt like he somehow knew Reef. The way he moved, the grace and style of an experienced snow-boarder who was purely in his element called to Ford. Underneath the bulky clothing, he could see how Reef moved his body to control everything about his slide down the slope.

"How you holding up, Reef?" Ford asked into his headset.

"I'm good. Go faster if you want. I can keep up."

"Let's do it, then." Ford crouched further, bending his legs and doubling over so his chest was almost resting on his thighs. Ski poles tucked under his arms, he shot forward. He could see Reef out of the corner of his eye as he cut from left to right behind him as they bee-lined for the pass up ahead. Ford looked up, watching the clouds pitch and roll overhead like stormy seas, darkening the previously blue sky and descending on them fast. Snow fall was getting heavier by the second. The temperature dropped quickly and with the stronger wind, the persistent cold that goes hand in hand with a whiteout had set in. Ford calculated they had about twenty minutes before visibility would be virtually zero.

"Ford, after we get over the pass how long will it take us to get to the ranger's hut?"

"Half hour maybe, although at this speed, less."

"We won't make it before the weather really sets in, will we?"

"No. I've never seen a front move this fast."

"You got rope or something we can tie ourselves together with?"

"No, but we can use one of my poles. I'll attach a wrist strap to each end so we can both hold on."

"Okay."

BY THE TIME they'd made it half way over the pass,

Ford was cursing that he hadn't chosen a snowboard. His ski boots were rigid. With no movement in his ankles or feet, he had to waddle up the slope. It was a hard going, exhausting trudge uphill wading through snow which was thigh-deep in some spots, holding skis and poles above it while trying not to slip on the icy patches buried under the powder. Reef had fared better and had moved in front of Ford as they climbed. Ford still felt strangely protective of him, wanting to shelter the younger man from the elements. Trailing him closely, Ford stopped short when Reef turned to him and smiled. "You're giving me one hell of a ride, Ford."

Ford's mind immediately went to the gutter as he pictured Reef up close and personal. Shirtless. His big hands trailing over Ford's skin. *What the fuck?* "I am?" he choked out. He wasn't sure whether he was shocked and confused over Reef's remark or his reaction to Reef's words.

"Seriously, wasn't expecting to be travelling the mountain pass to Mordor today. I'm waiting for an elf, a wizard and a fuckin' gnome to pop out in front of me."

"A dwarf." Ford chuckled.

"What?"

"*Lord of the Rings* has a dwarf, not a gnome. Come

on, I'm picturing two hot cups of tea with our names on them. Let's get off this pass so we can get out of this weather." Ford clamped his arm around Reef's shoulder and squeezed. He wasn't the sort of guy that hugged his friends often, but he needed the reassurance as much as he sensed Reef did. He knew he'd guessed correctly when Reef leaned his head momentarily against his. Reef's inch or two height advantage over Ford wasn't as obvious as it had been in the heli-tour company's offices when they'd been introduced, before either of them had put their boots on.

"Coffee, dude. You Brit's are all 'cups of tea' this and 'scones' that. But yeah, let's go." He flashed another grin at Ford, Reef's dimples showing through the dark-blond stubble on his cheeks.

They climbed in silence for another ten minutes until their steps faltered. The wind howled between the high cliffs on either side of them, pushing them to their knees. Ford had to get them to shelter. Had to protect Reef. The wind whistled too loud for them to speak, the biting cold cutting through Ford's layers of thermal clothing. Shivering, Ford put a hand on Reef's back, nudging him forward. They had to keep moving. He had to get them to the other side of the pass before they got too cold. Crawling up the final steepest most exposed part of the pass, Ford felt rather than saw the crest of the ridge. He pushed forward, guiding Reef to the high rock wall to shelter them.

As soon as Ford pulled them against the icy rocks, the swirling wind died down just enough that they could take a breath. He turned Reef toward him and squeezed his biceps through the thick material of his jacket. "How cold are you?" he shouted.

"Fuckin' freezing."

"Dizzy? Feel uncoordinated? Nauseous?" Ford questioned.

"No, I'm good. But we can't sit around here. Let's go."

"Hold up. The cabin is still a while away yet. Can you make it? If you've got any symptoms of hypothermia I'm gonna have to build a snow cave."

"I don't wanna get stuck out here, man. I'm good. I can make it."

"Let's strap in. We can ski the rest of the way. We're on the home stretch." Ford squeezed Reef's bicep encouragingly with his gloved hand.

"Thank fuck."

Ford dropped his skis to the sleet covered ground, and locked his booted feet in. Undoing the wrist strap, he looped it around the base of the other ski pole, creating a handle at either end. "I need you to wrap this around your wrist, Reef. Whatever you do, don't unhook it. Visibility is shithouse. I don't know if I'll find you if we get separated."

"Don't you let go either, dude."

Reef bent and closed the bindings, fixing his boots to his snowboard. Gripping the pole they nodded at each other and Ford pushed off, starting slowly as they got used to skiing while connected. It was difficult at best. Both needed to zigzag to control their speed, but being joined caused Ford to slingshot Reef as he passed in a wider arc around him. Ford respected the hell out of the guy's talent. He never once looked like he was struggling for balance even as they tentatively learned how to move together.

Whiteness blanketed them. Ford could barely see ten feet in front of himself. He was relying solely on his compass and altimeter to guide them to the ranger's hut. He silently sent up a prayer to the snow gods that he was heading in the right direction. It'd been a few seasons since he'd travelled over the pass to get to the station. Most other times he'd taken the tracks around the mountain, which if he calculated correctly, were directly in front of him on the other side of the valley they were travelling into.

He flexed his fingers trying to return some of the circulation to them. They were numb, the chill from the snow having seeped through the gloves while he crawled over the crest of the pass. Come to think of it, his toes were numb too. Ford checked the time on his watch once more. They were moving too slowly, but there was the odd rocky outcrop that they would have no hope of missing if they went any faster. Exposure in this weather for much longer would kill them. Ford pushed on knowing they had no other option but to go forward.

CHAPTER THREE

REEF LOOKED through the orange lenses of his goggles, and squinted. Monochrome orange. Everywhere. Visibility was so low that from Reef's vantage point – the length of the ski pole away – Ford was blurry, thick snowflakes filling the air between them. The sky had closed in even more, the clouds hanging so low that the fog was combining with snowflakes to create an almost impenetrable blanket of white. This was so not what he was used to. Snowboarding may have the label of an extreme sport, but it was controlled. Corporate sponsors and health and safety requirements, for both competitors and spectators mandated that runs were pre-checked with even freestyle courses being marked out carefully. He may spend his life in the snow, but Reef was pretty far out of his comfort zone. Those harsh Vermont winters he'd experienced as a kid came roaring back to him now.

Reef sucked in a breath and kept following Ford's lead. The dude was cool and calm under pressure, stopping to check on him regularly while pushing forward relentlessly. He barely knew him, but somehow that didn't matter. Reef instinctively knew he could rely on Ford to guide them out of this. And that confidence wasn't just because Ford was right next to him in the same danger Reef was. It was something much more than that – an innate knowledge that Ford wouldn't let him down.

How long had they been skiing? Surely they were close now. Reef's body was lagging, totally sapped of energy and he was disoriented – he felt like they were going in circles. The howling wind and freezing conditions weren't helping. Bone deep cold was setting in fast.

When Ford stopped in his tracks and pointed ahead Reef barely caught himself, halting only a millisecond before he yanked on Ford's arm which would have sent them both face first into the snow. Reef squinted and made out the straight walls and a tiny veranda against the sloping landscape. Snow had collected against the unprotected exterior, nearly burying the walls to the windowsills.

"Is this the place?" Reef looked at Ford. Seeing his nod, Reef couldn't hold back the grin on his lips.

"Come on, let's go," Ford whooped as he started to ski forward. Reef followed, disbelieving their luck at finding the hut right when they needed it.

The shovel hanging beside the door came in handy. Exhausted from the cold, tense trip, Reef struggled to clear enough snow to open the door while Ford dug out the firewood from the drift which had piled against it. At least whoever had carried the cut logs to the veranda had covered them with heavy waterproof canvass, ensuring they'd be usable by any winter visitors.

Stumbling into the hut, there wasn't much Reef needed to take in. The tiny kitchenette to the left consisted of a sink which sat on a wide cabinet, and an ice box. Straight ahead, past the kitchen, was a tiny two-seater sofa and a surprisingly large claw-foot tub, both situated in front of the open fireplace. Against the opposite wall stood a twin bunk bed with blankets neatly folded on the bottom tier. Ford bumped into Reef as he stepped in behind him, his arms full of the logs that would soon be burning in the fireplace and kicked the door closed behind them.

Glad to be out of the frigid conditions, Reef took some of the wood from Ford's hands and moved over to the fireplace with him. As Ford lit the smaller twigs and got a fire burning, Reef opened the flu on the chimney. As soon as it was burning in earnest, Ford added some of the larger logs to the pit. It was still freezing inside the station, but the fire and the lack of wind howling around them made it much more bearable.

"We need to get out of these wet clothes, get them in front of the fire to dry them."

"We'll freeze if we strip down to nothing now," Reef huffed as they stood.

"There's always an emergency pack with a few changes of dry thermals in one of the cupboards. We started adding them when we had a ranger fall into the stream nearby a couple of years ago. He had to sit wrapped in a blanket in front of the fire for hours until his clothes dried."

"Hey, listen, I... thank you. Without you, I would have been screwed. You saved my ass." Ford studied Reef for only a moment before pulling him into a hug. Reef wrapped his arms around Ford's waist and held tight, anchoring himself to the solid man before him. Burying his face in the crook of Ford's neck, he fought to drive down the lump in his throat and get his shaking under control. The adrenaline was wearing off fast, leaving him an emotional wreck.

"It's okay. You're safe. We both are. Deep breaths,

Reef. You're okay. You're okay." Ford's murmured words calmed him as he held Reef tight with one arm, rubbing his back with the other hand.

"Shit, dude, I'm sorry," Reef mumbled hoping that the stinging in his eyes wasn't caused by tears threatening to fall.

"Nothing to be sorry for," Ford whispered, his warm breath ghosting across Reef's cold throat. It was such an intimate position, but it felt so right. This contact, the connection between him and Ford was comforting, but as Reef tightened his grip around Ford's waist Ford's breath hitched. Awareness roared through Reef, stiffening his cock and quickening his breaths too. Ford's reaction was infinitesimal, but the strength of his embrace calmed Reef and lit his body on fire at the same time. Adrenaline. That's what it was. It had to be.

Reef loosened his grip and pulled back, Ford immediately did the same. The moment having passed, both men grinned and stepped away from each other.

"Before we get out of our gear, wanna help me shovel some snow into the water heater? It'll warm up pretty quick and we can each have a soak if we don't fill the tub up too much."

"Yeah? Where is it?"

"Right there." Ford pointed to the pipes forming

the base of the fireplace feeding into the tank. "We turn this lever and it circulates the water through the pipes, heating it. Then we just empty it into the tub when it's hot enough. It's surprisingly effective."

"Fuckin' genius," Reef murmured, following the path of the pipes into the heater before going outside with Ford to shovel some snow.

"Holy shit, it's cold out here," Ford gasped. A full body shudder wracked Reef when the full force of the wind hit him as he stepped off the veranda. Fifteen minutes later, nearly an inch of the powdery flakes had blown back onto the timber planks. They moved enough buckets into the heater to fill it, the ice inside melting fast. Topping another two pails, they carried them inside and shut the door, kicking off their boots as they entered. The bare timber floor was cold under Reef's thermal socks.

"Come on, you need to get warm," Ford prompted. "Get that wet gear off. I'll put some tea on."

"Dude, really? Tea?" Reef chuckled.

"Urgh, fine. Coffee. Hope you don't mind it black."

"At this point, I'll take it however it comes." Reef stripped out of his jacket and turned the lever, circulating the water through the heater.

"You can check the temperature on the gauge on

the front of the heater. Just give it a second to adjust to the right level after you've stirred up the water."

"Ah, Ford? It's in Celsius?"

"Sixty degrees is hot enough for a soak."

———

FORD PULLED out the mugs and surveyed what food there was. *Damn, no tea bags.* He was having a hard time resisting the temptation of stealing a glance at Reef. He had no idea what had gotten into him. When Reef had thanked him, tears had stung Ford's eyes. The stress and fear from the day had come crashing down onto his shoulders and he'd almost buckled under the pressure. Ford had reached out and grabbed onto Reef, but Reef's arms around him had done something completely unexpected. The strong embrace had stripped away all the bad, and in its place desire had roared in, hot and thick like lava. His body shuddered and his dick hardened impossibly. He had to fight like the devil to stop himself rutting against the man. The most daunting part about it was that Ford wasn't scared, or worried, or even concerned. It had felt too... right. What the hell was wrong with him? Reef was a dude. But as Ford pondered that nugget of obviousness, he couldn't help but acknowledge that Reef had his interest, and his dick, piqued.

And he'd smelled so good. Like the outdoors... and man.

Fuck! Stop it.

Using the thick mitt hanging next to the fireplace, Ford took the whistling kettle off the hook over the roaring fire and stepped back to the kitchen, desperately trying to ignore the man currently laying his ski pants out on the stone surrounding the fireplace. He'd caught a glimpse of the pale skin on Reef's back above his black briefs. Ford had diverted his eyes immediately.

"Oh hell yeah," Reef groaned as Ford heard the water sloshing in the bath. "Fuckin' heaven."

"I'll leave your coffee on the counter for you, Reef."

"What do I have to do to get you to bring it to me?"

Ford's body tightened more, his cock throbbed as a bead of pre-cum wet the material of his boxers. Turning away he adjusted himself, hoping the loose ski pants he still wore hid the evidence of his arousal. Sucking in a breath at the pressure on his cock, Ford struggled not to moan. *What the hell is happening?* He steeled himself and walked to Reef, handing the mug to him. Ford kept his gaze locked on the other man's face. The grin which Reef shot Ford was pure wickedness.

"Just ask," he croaked out.

"Thanks, buddy. So, what are we gonna do for the rest of the day?" Reef asked as he sipped his coffee.

Ford sat on the sofa and watched Reef, shirtless and lying back in the tub. Head resting on the rim, his back arched pushing the ripped muscles of his lean chest forward. "Ah..." Ford lost the ability to speak, a condition which as a perpetual flirt he'd never suffered from before.

"Twenty questions it is then. How long have you been a heli-guide for?" Reef asked, seemingly oblivious to Ford's condition.

Clearing his throat, Ford spoke up. "This is my first day." At Reef's wide-eyed, open-mouthed look, Ford laughed. "I'm not a guide. I'm mountain rescue. I do the occasional guided tour because it's easier to jump down and ski a back trail to take a look at the avalanche zones than it is for me to hike up."

"Holy shit. I guess I was damn lucky getting you then."

"What do you do for a living?" Ford asked, taking a sip of coffee and cringing. "This shit is disgusting. How can you drink it?" Ford put the mug on the floor of the cabin and unzipped his jacket, stripping it off.

He looked up, waiting for Reef's response. "It's the nectar of life, my friend." Raising his mug to toast Ford, Reef continued, "Although this instant shit *is* awful. I'm a pro-snowboarder."

He looked blankly at Reef for a moment, before all the puzzle pieces fell into place and he recognized that wicked grin. Ford slapped his hand across his forehead. "Fuck me. You're Reef Reid." He was a fan. A big one. Had been for years. Reef's moves on the snow were a thing of beauty. Precision jumps and flawless landings. He couldn't figure out why the man hadn't won the World Championship yet. Ford knew it was just a matter of time before the younger man held that title. Carrying his discarded jacket, Ford laid it and his ski pants before the fire. Dressed only in his thermal t-shirt and knee length tight boxer shorts, he sprawled out on the sofa again.

"Yep, last time I checked. How long have you lived in New Zealand?"

"I feel like a complete dumbass. I've followed your career for years." As Reef raised his mug smiling at him, Ford shook his head and continued, "Um, New Zealand, right. I live here part time. I spend ski season here, then fly back to Europe and do winter in Italy. When I'm between seasons, I normally head to my parents' estate in the South of France."

"You hang with your folks during your downtime?"

"No, they only make the trip from the UK for a couple of weeks each year. I have the place to myself more often than not. And when they're there, I stay in the guest house. Ah, single or in a relationship?"

A cloud descended over Reef's features. "Recently single. You?"

Ford chuckled. "I'm very much single."

"Why?"

"Why pick one menu item when I can sample everything? I'm guessing you prefer reheating the same meal over and over."

"Bad analogy, dude. But, no, I've never really done casual sex." Holding up his hand and shaking his head, Reef stopped Ford's question before he could blurt it out. "I get it, I get it. I'm a guy. I like sex, I fucking love it. I could pick up the snow bunnies that follow us along the circuit, but even though I could, I guess I don't. For me, sex is better if it means something."

Ford sat quietly looking at Reef, absorbing what he said. Their eyes met and held, and Ford's body responded, heating and hardening. "Your question," he choked out.

"Do you want a soak?"

"Huh?"

"Do you want to hop in the tub? I'm ready to get out."

"Ah, yeah." Ford nodded. Reef stood and reached for the towel stacked near the tub. Ford's breath hitched as what he could only describe as unbridled lust ripped through him. Reef was long and lean, a couple of inches taller than his own six foot two inch height. Reef's broad shoulders and defined pecs tapered to a slim waist. And that happy trail? It lead to a patch of dark-blond hair framing a cock that was long and thick. *Is he sporting a semi?* The muscles in Reef's long legs rippled as he shifted his weight, shaking out the towel and wrapping it around his waist. Stepping out of the tub, Reef turned and pulled the plug out, draining the water. Ford's gaze zeroed in on his tight ass. Damn, there were no words to describe it. It was... perfect.

What the fuck? Ford was sitting there drooling over another dude. A fucking perfect specimen of a man, but still, a dude. Adrenaline was a fucked up son of a bitch. *I'm in a whiteout and suddenly I'm hot for Reef Reid? What in the hell am I thinking?*

———

REEF MADE a quick exit from the tub and walked

straight over to the twin bunks where the two sets of thermal long-johns were laid out. Ford had found them in the well-stocked hut, just as he'd anticipated. He and Ford would each have to wash and dry their own gear before wearing it again.

He pulled on the too-big thermals and headed over to the sole cupboard in the small cabin. Reef needed some distance between he and Ford. He'd been trapped in the tub with an erection that was as hard as stone, powerless to stop staring at Ford as he slowly removed each piece of his ski gear. Peeling off the heavy outer layer of clothing left Ford in nothing but a tight-fitting shirt and knee-length shorts which molded to every ridge and hollow in the man's ripped body. *Since when are thermals sexy?* Apparently since Ford gave him an impromptu and sexy-as-fuck strip tease. His pecs, abs, lats and biceps were all perfectly defined even under the shirt. Reef had always appreciated a good body—Addilyn had pointed out enough of those she considered perfect specimens—but he was admiring Ford's from a whole new perspective. Reef found him sexy in a way he'd never imagined. Ford was a *man's* man. A touch shorter than Reef, but brawnier. And those blue eyes and chocolate brown hair? Revelatory. Mussed up from their helmets, Ford's curls called to him. Reef had never had such an irresistible urge to run his fingers through anyone's hair like he had the moment he watched Ford do it. *Is it as soft as it looks?*

Reef had his fingers tightly clamped around his cock the whole time he was in the tub trying to tame his erection. Watching Ford sprawl out on the sofa, legs apart so that Reef's view was filled with that jealousy-inducing package was almost too much. Reef fought every instinct in his body, telling him to reach down and jack himself off until he blew everywhere. And now with Ford lying naked in the tub, the very same one that Reef was in only a moment ago, Reef's cock was back up saluting the world. Being in a confined space with the man was going to test his restraint.

What the hell is wrong with me?

He wasn't attracted to men. Well, he wasn't, until Ford. Okay, so maybe Reef had crushed a little on his snowboarding hero. The man had taken him under his wing during Reef's first few years on the pro-tour, but compared to this it was barely worth mentioning. There was nowhere near the level of attraction back then to what he felt now. Reef shook his head. The way his body reacted made it impossible to argue that he wasn't sexually attracted to Ford—

"Dude, what's your surname? You never told me."

"Wallace."

"Cool."

Still staring at the two cans of lamb and vegetable stew and the pot which Ford had pulled out of the cupboards, Reef pulled himself together, opened the pull-tabs and dumped the contents in the pot. Carrying it over to the fireplace, Reef caved and stole a glance at Ford. Dark hair dusted perfectly formed pecs glistening with water droplets and continued like a roadmap down his ripped abs. Reef tore his gaze away and took a deep breath, grinding his teeth together. It took all Reef's strength to stop himself from climbing in the tub and licking those drops sliding down Ford's skin.

Faaark!

Reef needed to get his head on straight. There was no way it would end well if he didn't get his body under control. He replayed their conversation, desperate to come up with something that would put them in safe territory again. Ford's parents. That was it.

"So, your parents have a place in the South of France? What's it like? What are they like?"

"The place is beautiful. Hills, grape vines, little villages with cobblestone roads, great cafés, hot women. What more could you want? My parents? That's a harder question. I remember them as madly in love when I was growing up. But then something happened. Neither of them talk about it, but their relationship hasn't been the same since. Now it's like Father tolerates Mother, and Mother is a cold-hearted bitch. He's even more of a workaholic than when I was a kid, and that's saying something. It's all very tense and uncomfortable."

"Shit, sorry man. That sucks." Reef turned back to the stew he was absently stirring.

"Don't be. I've spent enough time trying to talk to them, to get them to open up, but they just change the subject. I figure it's their life, not mine. If they want things to change, they'll make it happen. What about yours?"

Reef shook his head. His family was a fucked up mess. "Petal and River are hippies born into the wrong generation. They're all about free love and getting on the road. They smoke way too much weed and have zero sense of responsibility. They're clueless. It's been a few years since I've seen them. I went home a while ago, but apparently they were inspired to go to Arizona so I missed them."

"Did you try to surprise them?"

Looking over his shoulder at Ford, Reef shook his head and shrugged. He'd long ago given up trying to rationalize their behavior. His parents were off in their own little world and barely surfaced long enough to realize they'd hurt him, yet again. "No, I'd organized it with them weeks earlier. Like I said, zero responsibility."

"Dude, I can't believe that."

"Eh, it's not like I don't talk to them anymore, but they aren't your typical parents. Momma Bear and Coach are more like that for me."

"Who's that?"

Reef smiled. Coach and Momma Bear were his constants. They were exactly what he wanted in life, love that lasted decades and only grew stronger through the tough parts, a home, a tight circle of friends and family. He wanted suburbia, kids, the dog, the white picket fence. "Coach trains the football team at the school I went to. Momma Bear is his wife."

"So you played football?"

"Hell no, I was always too small for that." Reef laughed remembering his first night at their house. "When I was thirteen I got my first entry into a comp. Mom booked my flights but forgot my accommodation. When I got there, I didn't know what to do. I called them, but they'd gone to some music festival so they weren't contactable. I don't really have any other family, so I called my best friend. He put his Mom on and she called the school thinking it was something they might have set up. The office called Coach. Of course, I had nothing to do with the football team so Coach called Momma Bear to see if she could sort me out. She was horrified. Got me into a hotel, flew out to watch me, then took me home with her when we got back."

Reef took the bubbling pot of stew off the hook above the fire. For canned food, it smelled pretty good. Ladling it into the bowls he'd brought over, Reef passed one to Ford.

"I don't even know what to say to that," Ford said as he took the spoon Reef held out.

"Thanks?"

"Smartass." Ford grinned at him. "Thank you." By the time Reef sat on the sofa cradling the bowl, Ford had a towel wrapped around his waist and was stepping out of the tub.

"Momma Bear took good care of me. Coach did too." Reef smiled again. "That first night I was at their house, he looked me up and down and got pissed. I thought I was in major trouble until he told me I needed to fatten myself up so I didn't freeze out on the ski field. I was at Coach and Momma Bear's house for two weeks after the comp and did nothing but eat the whole time."

"Your parents were away for a few weeks?"

"Most of it." Reef nodded.

"Un-fucking-believable. Sorry, I don't mean to bad-mouth your parents, but that's neglect," Ford commented with a healthy dose of disgust in his voice as he seated himself on the small sofa, his thigh pressing against Reef's.

"Probably. Momma Bear says the same thing. It's just how it was." Reef shrugged. "We were always together when I was little. But then I grew up a bit and told them that I wanted to go to school, and live in a house like a regular kid. They figured out that I hated their lifestyle and decided to keep on doing it without me. They'd only been leaving me alone for about six months when I got into my first comp. After that, I spent most of my time at Momma Bear and Coach's."

"So you got along with their kids?" Ford asked as he placed his empty bowl on the coffee table. Reef followed, stacking his on top before leaning back into the cushions.

"They don't have any. They tried for years but no luck. I kinda became their adopted kid."

"You were lucky."

"Unbelievably. They saved me in more ways than one."

They fell silent then, watching the flames in the fireplace as they listened to the whistling of the wind outside the cozy cabin.

CHAPTER FOUR

FORD LISTENED to the sounds around them. The fire and the roaring wind seemed to fade into the background as he found himself focusing on the man sitting next to him. With every breath Reef took, Ford became more aware of Reef's chest rising and falling, his fingers tapping a slow rhythm on his leg and the laid back pose that had Reef's thigh pressing against his own on the too-small sofa. When he exhaled on a long, slow breath Ford turned to him, his lips quirking up at the man's closed eyes and dreamy smile.

"You look like you're falling asleep," Ford murmured.

Opening one eye and cocking a brow at him, Reef grinned. "Nah, just relaxed. Been so long since I've just sat and stopped for a minute. I have nowhere to be for a couple of months. No pressure. I'm just here in the moment with you. I haven't had that in forever. I don't know if I've ever had that, I've always had a competition or training coming up, travelling to do. It's nice."

"Yeah, must be. How'd you manage to swing a season off with your sponsors? Have you lost them?"

"Normally that's what'd happen but I was damn lucky. Been with them since the beginning; I suppose they were paying back my loyalty. Momma Bear suggested that I have some time off to recharge, so I did. She could see how burnt out I've been. I've pushed pretty hard, but I felt like I needed to, you know? Probably a good thing I did, too."

"Yeah?"

"Addilyn – my ex – wanted me to stop training so I could follow her around in the off-season. Now I'm glad I didn't."

"You two were dating up until recently, weren't you? Media were all over it when you split."

"Yeah, was a bit of a circus for a while. I knew it would be, but I wasn't gonna stick around after she cheated."

"No," Ford exclaimed, unbelieving. Why the fuck would she cheat on Reef? He was... was... hell, he was fuckin' sexy and a good guy and he worked hard. He dug... no wait, chicks dug that. Didn't they?

"Blamed it on me because I didn't make the effort to go see her."

"What, she couldn't come to you?" he asked disgusted.

"She hates cold weather."

"So? Put a fuckin' jacket on. What a bitch."

"You said it." Reef was scowling now, pain and anger clearly written in his expression – his mouth tight, his eyes downcast. Reef was so laid back. How did he even end up dating such a high-maintenance girl? He didn't deserve her shit. Fuckin' supermodels. Addilyn Knight was notorious, almost as bad as that other one who lost it a few years earlier and started throwing shit at people.

Reef sighed and cracked his knuckles, looking away from Ford as he did so. Ford's outrage at the way Reef's ex had treated him evaporated, leaving Ford hurting for his new friend. How was it he felt so close to a man whom he barely knew? The inexplicable protective streak flared through Ford again as he reached out to comfort Reef, hesitating when he was only an inch away from grasping his shoulder. *Is this the right thing to do? Yes, yes it is.*

"So... twenty questions. I think it's your turn,

buddy," Ford prompted as his hand closed around Reef's shoulder and he squeezed. Reef's smile, although small, lit up the room. Ford couldn't help but grin back.

"Right, my question." Reef answered, his smile growing. "Damn, where's the tequila when you need it?"

"What for?"

"Truth or drink. What else? Um, okay... let's make things interesting. Twosome, threesome or moresome?"

"Oh, so that's how we're playin' now?" Ford chuckled. "A couple of threesomes in college, but only twosomes since. You?"

"Dude, do you need to ask? I'm a relationship kinda guy. I only do twosomes. Doesn't mean that my sex life is boring though." Pausing he scratched his head and looked at Ford, understanding dawning in his eyes. "Or maybe it is. My hand and I are pretty damn well acquainted. I..." He shook his head. "Fuck me, that's why she did it, isn't it? She's out there living the high life, partying with the beautiful people and all I want is to snuggle on the sofa. I'm too boring."

"No, no way. This isn't on you. If she wasn't happy she should have spoken to you, not gone and shagged another dude. That's not on. This is on her."

"Dudes. Not just one; there were a few."

"It's all on her. How many years have Momma Bear and Coach been married and stayed faithful? And your mom and dad? She didn't deserve you."

"Momma Bear would like you. She said exactly the same thing about her." Reef knocked his elbow gently into Ford, leaning against him as they talked.

"She's a smart woman."

"Now you're just sucking up." Reef laughed.

"Got you smiling, didn't I?" Ford grinned, throwing an arm around Reef's shoulder. "If it makes you feel better, I can't get the girl I've been asking out forever because I don't date. She wants a relationship and I won't give her one."

"I'd tell you to introduce us, but that might get a little weird."

"Yeah, might be."

"You really like her, huh?"

Ford thought about it. He'd asked Shelly out every time they'd spoken; yet they hadn't actually met until four months after he'd first spoken with her. Did he like her? Maybe. Maybe it was that he knew he didn't have a chance – a bit of betting on a sure failure so he didn't have to commit to anything.

"Honestly? I don't know. As pathetic as it is to admit, I have no idea."

They'd spent the better part of the night talking,

asking stupid questions, laughing and sobering up with the much more serious ones. Ford cringed after he'd blurted out, "What do you want from life?" He had the sinking feeling that it'd just bring Reef down again. Before he and Addilyn split, he seemed to be on the way to having what any professional sportsperson would want: a rockin' career, close to being World Champion and a model to fuck.

The maturity of Reef's response flawed him: suburbia, kids, the dog, and a white picket fence. He knew that Reef wasn't your typical mid-twenty something man, but Ford supposed he'd underestimated him. Ford had joked that a picket fence – albeit a dark grey one – wasn't all it was cracked up to be. The one around his own cottage was a yearly pain in the ass to repaint. But Reef just smiled longingly. His love of domestic tasks baffled Ford but he understood why Reef yearned for it. He'd travelled almost non-stop for the last five years or so, never staying more than a month or so in one place. Settling down for him would probably be heaven.

The storm hadn't let up at all. Ford relaxed against the sofa, arm still around Reef as they listened to the creaking of the roof and the howling wind rattling both the single window and door with each strong gust. Both of them were falling asleep and neither would be in any shape to cross country ski the next day if they didn't get up. With one eye open, Ford eyed the twin bunks. Reef had made up the beds while Ford cleaned up after dinner. The beds were ready to go, but as uncomfortable as the sofa would be to sleep on, Reef's warm body pressed against his on the sofa was too hard to let go of. Wanting to enjoy their closeness a little longer, Ford ignored the cramps in his muscles from the small seat.

"Let's go to bed," Reef murmured, nuzzling into Ford's shoulder, already half asleep. "This sofa's awful; my ass is numb."

As much as Ford didn't want to move, he couldn't stay there knowing Reef was uncomfortable. Would it be weird if he suggested they sleep on the same bunk? Probably. "Yeah, come on. Top or bottom bunk?"

Sighing, Reef pulled himself away. "I'll go top. Wouldn't want you to strain a muscle getting up, old man."

"Hey, I'm eight years older than you. That's nothing."

"It's almost a decade."

"Fuck you." Ford laughed.

REEF LAID between the cool sheets on the top bunk, a blanket draped over his body. He was suddenly wide awake. He'd been cuddling with Ford on the sofa for hours. And it felt so right. Familiar. Comfortable. Reef had never connected with anyone so quickly, or so completely like that before. He supposed it must have something to do with the storm. Strangers making their way to safety in a blizzard, then being trapped together for what was going to be at least another day was make or break. They'd either become fast friends, or enemies. Thank the stars it was the friendship route they seemed to be taking. But that wasn't really the truth either. There was something more than friendship between them. It was crazy and Reef was conflicted.

He was as turned on as fuck.

Ford's body was a work of art. Reef's cock thickened at the memory of Ford's wet hair dripping rivulets of water from its straightened locks. Each drop glinted along his perfectly formed muscles as the dim light cast by the fire reflected off them. A soft huff of breath from below stole the image from his mind and replaced it with a far more erotic one. Want and need rushed through Reef, hardening his cock to steel.

Reef laid back watching Ford hover above him, glued to the sight of Ford closing his hand around his long thick cock, working his fist slowly up and down. Ford's muscles twitched and flexed, his back arching as their eyes locked. Reef moaned – louder than he could help – when he gripped his own steely length still clothed in the loose thermal pants he wore. Thrusting his hips into his fist, Reef squeezed. They traded grunts and groans as Reef tugged his cock free and began working it. Ford fell forward, caging him in with those strong arms and his heavy body. Reef's shirt disappeared. Skin against skin, lips on his as they ground against each other. Ford's stubble scraped against Reef's lips and tongue as he licked and bit a line from Ford's mouth to the sensitive spot below his ear.

Hardness under soft skin.

Heat.

The smell of sex in the air.

A wildfire curled low in his belly as Reef reached for Ford, running his hands over the smooth skin of Ford's back down to his tight ass. He gripped and pulled Ford against him harder, both of them panting. Sensation exploded through his body from their cocks sliding against each other, pre-cum lubricating their way. The bunk squeaked and a muffled grunt reached Reef's ears. Ford buried his face in the crook of Reef's neck. Then he was inside Reef, stretching him, filling him completely.

Ford thrust powerfully, their bodies connected as they moved as one.

Reef widened his legs, his hips lifting off the bed as his orgasm crashed over him. The tingles at the base of his spine exploded outwards and with each stroke of his fist hot semen pumped through him. Zings shot through every nerve in his body. The illicit fantasy of his guide licking those jets of cum from Reef's exposed belly and chest sent even more shudders through him, prolonging the ecstasy. Biting down on his forearm, Reef unsuccessfully tried to quiet the moans escaping his lips as his cock finally stopped shooting stripes of cum onto his body. He loosened his grip on his cock as the pulsing subsided, a post-orgasmic glow blanketed his body.

Sleep was rushing at him, but the cooling stickiness on his skin kept him connected with wakefulness. Ripping off the thermal shirt he'd borrowed, he wiped himself down and pulled the blankets over himself just as he heard Ford's breathing even out. Reef refused to let his mind takeover and dim the satisfied glow coursing through him. There'd be plenty of time in the morning for Reef to figure out what the hell was going on in his head. Ford was a dude – a damn sexy one, but still a dude. And Reef had just blown his load so hard, he was almost cross-eyed to visions of that man fucking him in the ass. It was a good thing they had hours of cross-country snowboarding in front of them. Reef was going to need every one of them, and more, to process what had just happened.

THREE NIGHTS. That's how long they'd been holed up in the cabin with no decent coffee. It was killing him. Ford grimaced every time he drank a cup and Reef had started to do it too. What he wouldn't give for a good cup of joe. Even the girly, non-fat soy latte with caramel and hazelnut shots and whipped cream and ice cream, or whatever the hell those drinks were, would be better than the crap they were drinking. And he couldn't even drown it in sweetener or cream. They didn't have any of that either.

"Here, honeybuns," Reef said as he handed the latest mug of stale instant coffee to Ford, joining him at the window to look out over the blanket of white.

"Thanks, sweet cheeks," Ford responded without missing a beat. They'd fallen into a teasing friendship in the last few days. Ford was an irrepressible flirt and Reef felt his pull being drawn in hook, line and sinker. Blowing the steam off the top of the mug, Ford took a tentative sip. "Urgh, doesn't get any better. I'm never drinking this pigswill again and I'm personally stocking all these bloody cabins with tea."

Reef chuckled, squeezing Ford's other shoulder. "Poor baby."

"Shut up," Ford grumbled, leaning into Reef as they watched the snow fall.

Food and firewood was beginning to run low and Reef was starting to pace. That was never a good thing. He wasn't used to staying indoors and doing nothing for so long. The furthest they'd travelled was to the side of the cabin to haul in buckets of fresh snow for melting and to the end of the porch to collect extra firewood. Reef was getting antsy.

Ford read him well, letting the comfortable silence envelop them, or dissipating tension with teasing. Both their cell phones had long since died and with no way of charging them at the cabin, were destined to stay that way. That meant no more tunes, but that was okay too. Reef had had the chance to think a lot about things these last few days. He wanted to settle down, sleep in the same bed, make friends with his neighbors. He was sick of travelling so much. He was a nomad, exactly like his parents. There was no avoiding the planes and airports, the trips up and down mountains, hotel food and living out of a suitcase during competition season, but Reef had had enough of the year-round training.

Ford's idea of splitting his life between two countries inspired Reef to think about the same. If he did that maybe, just maybe, he'd get to have what he always wanted out of life.

"The storm's slowed. I think the worst is behind us," Ford said quietly from beside him.

"Looks like it. You think it's safe to leave yet?"

"Yeah, think so. We have a full day's hike ahead of us to get to the pickup spot, and we don't have the right gear, so it's gonna take longer. If we leave it much later, it'll be too dark for them to come and get us."

"Okay then, let's get packed up and dressed."

REEF PULLED his goggles down over his helmet and picked up his snowboard, trudging further up the slope as they both tried to get through to base on their helmet-mounted radios again. "Nada. Still." They'd been trying for two hours, hiking steadily up the slope away from the cabin. Dread curled in Reef's gut. It didn't feel right. Surely they should have been able to get through by now. The sky had cleared in the couple of hours they'd been outside, the clouds starting to break apart and the glorious blue sky peeping through. These were the best conditions to snowboard in. A massive dump of fresh powder, relatively warm weather compared to the last couple of days' freezing temperatures and no people to get in his way. The problem was, they'd be stuck out here until either the chopper or mountain rescue could get to them. If they didn't get through soon, they'd have to turn and head back to the cabin to wait out the night and with the fire-wood getting low they were going to be cold.

"I'm gonna head up a little higher. I'm getting something on the radio, but it's not clear enough."

"Alright man, I need to take off my boot and fix up my sock." They bumped fists and Reef watched Ford maneuver his skis and trudge up the slope toward an outcropping of rocks. Time slowed to a crawl as the crack, crack, crack of the slope giving way underneath Ford's feet smashed through the silence of the mountain around them. Reef shouted, and ran the fifty, or so, feet toward him; his movements slowed in the thigh deep powder. It was like he was anchored in quick-sand. Reef reached out willing his arm to stretch to an impossible length, as he desperately tried to grab a finger hold of his friend's ski pole. Ford had pivoted, skiing back toward Reef like a mad man.

He was too far away.

Ford pushed forward with powerful movements; but his attempt to pick up speed and get out of the way of the slipping slope was futile. Reef read the fear on

Ford's mostly covered face as the vital seconds ticked by.

"Ford, hurry up. Please," Reef begged, shouting over the roaring of the snow careening down the mountain. The noise, as loud as a jet engine, drowned out his pleas as Ford moved closer to him. They were barely an arm's length apart as Reef's worst nightmare unfolded before his eyes. Ford stumbled, the snow shifting beneath his feet quicker now as the tsunami of white picked him up and tossed him like a ragdoll, hurtling him down the steep gradient. Reef reacted on instinct, running after the man that had, in four days, come to mean more to him than any friend he'd ever had. His eyes locked on the churning mass of snow, Reef frantically looking for any sign of Ford.

Calling his name over and over again Reef searched, scanning every inch of the still snow before him. He had no idea how long he'd been looking. Minutes could have turned into hours, but Reef couldn't give up hope. He wouldn't. Was Ford alive? He didn't pray to a god, but right then he would have done anything, including hand his soul over to the Devil himself, if it meant he could save Ford. "Please," he whispered, his voice hoarse from shouting.

Then he was there.

Ford's boot stuck out of the snow, the black of his

ski pants contrasting against the perfect white back-drop. Any other time, or any other day, Reef would have admired the beauty and raw power of nature. But the diamond-like sparkle of the snow crystals reflecting the sun were ignored as Reef frantically dug Ford's life-less body out of the snow. Tears streamed down his face as he reached the junction of Ford's knee, bent at an awkward angle. *Was it broken?*

"Please, please be alive. I'm here Ford. I have you. I'll get you out of this mess. Please just be okay." The red of Ford's jacket was uncovered and Reef ran his gloved hands up the length of his body until he reached the collar of the thick material. Using all his strength, Reef hauled on Ford's jacket lifting him out of, what would become, his snowy grave unless he could breathe. And soon.

Ford's goggles and mic had been torn off, lost to the elements, but his helmet was still strapped tight to his chin. Flicking open the clasp, Reef tugged it off and tossed it aside. He leaned down close, checking Ford's breathing. But there was nothing. No puff of warm air against his cheek. Scrambling, Reef yanked off his own helmet while feeling Ford's throat for a heart rate. Weak beats pulsed against his fingers. He was alive, but hurt. And not breathing.

Tossing his own helmet aside, he tilted Ford's head

back and held open his mouth, Reef performing mouth to mouth on him. Five, six, seven times before Reef watched Ford's chest rise on his own accord. Relief flooded through him, ripping a raw sob from his throat. Cradling Ford's head, Reef leaned down and closed his eyes, nestling against the crook of Ford's neck.

Ford's moan had Reef pulling back slightly. "Re... Re..." he choked out.

"Shh," Reef murmured as he stroked Ford's cheek. "I've got you. I'm gonna carry you back to the cabin." Reef ran his hands over Ford's body, checking for any other broken bones and sore spots. Finding none other than his knee, he paused looking at Ford and took a deep breath to steady his emotions.

Ford brought his hands to Reef's hair and brushed the snow that had fallen in the blond strands. "You saved me," he whispered.

"I was so fuckin' scared. I thought I'd lost you."

Ford's eyes drifted to Reef's mouth and he licked his bottom lip. That lick was the sexiest thing Reef had ever seen and he found himself being tugged toward Ford by an invisible tractor beam. He was sure his own expression matched Ford's, whose lids dropped to half-mast as their gaze collided and the chemistry between them exploded in a fireworks display. Lips barely a hair's breadth away from each other, they startled apart when the plaintive kee-a of a hawk sounded from high above them. The moment lost, Reef wrapped Ford's arm around his shoulders, sat back on his haunches and pulled him into a sitting position.

"Think you can stand if I support your weight? I'm not so good at dead lifting grown men."

Ford chuckled and nodded. "Yeah," he murmured, his voice returning stronger. "I can walk. I'll use my poles to steady me."

"Not gonna happen, and don't argue. Let me do this."

CHAPTER FIVE

THE TREK back to the ranger's hut was the longest, slowest walk of Ford's life. In fact, his entire thirty-three years of life felt shorter than the bloody hike he'd made, not that he'd taken a single step of it. Ford had spent the entire trip in a fireman's hold over Reef's shoulder. And he felt like shit. Leaving all the work to Reef ate away at Ford. *He* was the one who should be doing that job, but instead he was laid up because of a... okay, well it *was* an avalanche. Ford let out a snort of laughter, causing Reef to pause. "You okay there?"

"Yeah, I'm pissed that an avalanche laid me up, and then I thought about how ridiculous that sounds."

Reef bent so Ford's good leg could support his weight on the ground. Keeping a hold of him, Reef stood so they were face to face. Those warm brown eyes gazed at Ford and drew him in. They'd had to stop more times than he could count to give Reef a bit of a rest and help Ford beat the pain of his screaming knee back to a level where he could bear to be lifted into Reef's arms again. Reef had stumbled along a particularly steep part of the mountain, dropping onto one knee in a lunge. He kept a tight hold of Ford as he pushed up. Any person who hadn't spent half their life on the snow balancing on a board would have struggled to stay upright, but Reef did it. Ford squeezed Reef's shoulders and smiled at him. What he really wanted to do was kiss those lips, like he'd nearly done before, but he was too much of a chicken shit to admit it out loud.

"Thank you for saving me."

"You've already said that. And there was no way I was leaving until I carried your ass outta there. And, I'm not drinking bad coffee alone." The emotion behind Reef's words betrayed his flippant comment. He gave Ford a small smile, those dimples barely showing. Ford couldn't stand the distance between them anymore and pulled Reef to him, hugging him tightly in the knee-deep snow. He may not be man enough to kiss him, but he couldn't keep away when Reef's bravery and heroism rivalled that of any superhero. The bone deep cold soaking through his wet gear and thermals and the pain in his leg evaporated in that instant, replaced with Reef's presence in his arms. This man had saved him. Then he'd carried him for hours without ever complaining, navigating slopes so steep in some places that they'd be classified as runs reserved for experts in a ski resort.

"Come on, let's keep going. You're too cold to stay out here." As each step had progressed, Reef had slowed, looking exhausted as he bent to pick up Ford again.

Stopping him before he lifted him, Ford laid a hand on his shoulder and said, "Let me walk, Reef."

"I don't want you to hurt yourself more," he replied through clenched teeth as he lifted Ford, stumbling and pitching them forward. They were sent sprawling in the snow less than a hundred yards from the cabin. Ford shouted out in pain, while Reef cussed a blue streak.

Clutching his thigh above his bruised and swollen knee, Ford fought back the urge to puke.

"Fuck, I'm so sorry. Damn, you're hurting so bad. Isn't there anything in your pack you can take?"

"Yeah," he groaned. "Gimme anything you can find. I can't wait any longer." Reef pulled Ford's glove down to expose his wrist, unscrewed the dial on his watch and pulled the antenna out, finally activating the emergency GPS. Ford had told him to hold off, to wait until they were on safer ground and closer to a possible chopper landing point than they were in the avalanche zone. But now, even Ford could see that he was in trouble.

Reef pulled off the pack that he'd been carrying and rifled around in its contents until he found the strongest pain killers Ford kept with him. Taking the pills from him, Ford waited for Reef to pass him the flask of water from his jacket.

The cold of the snow surrounding him was seeping into Ford's bones and the shivering that had begun earlier was now setting in in earnest. Ford struggled to keep his eyes open, the warmth and peacefulness of sleep beckoning him.

"I need to lift you. You're going into shock or have hypothermia or something. I need to get you warm." Ford nodded. He had nothing left, exhaustion sweeping over him as the pain numbed his awareness. "Stay with me, Ford. Stay awake. Come on, please, buddy. Open your eyes," Reef's constant encouragement as he trudged the remaining distance to the ranger's station had Ford's eyes fluttering open momentarily, and a weak smile lifting his lips as Reef carried him like a bride over the threshold and into the cabin.

Reef laid him down gently onto the sofa and began taking off his soaked jacket. His strong hands lifted

Ford's body up and he pulled down the sleeves, taking it off him. Cool fingertips trailed up his body as Reef lifted the soaked thermal t-shirt Ford wore underneath and maneuvered it over his head and arms. Those fingertips returned, gently caressing the bruises forming on Ford's ribs before moving efficiently to his ski boots.

It didn't matter that Reef had years of experience in the snow, a person could only be so gentle taking ski boots off. Even the best quality ones like Ford's were a bitch to pull off. Snug fitting to mid-calf, it usually took a few good tugs to get them over a person's heel. Ford was suddenly very awake with the knowledge of what was coming. He'd taken off countless boots in order to stabilize ankles, knees and hips – and all the muscles between – hurt on the groomed fields he patrolled. He sucked in a breath and gladly took the glove that Reef handed him between his teeth. Biting down on it, Ford tried to distract himself from the pain. A strong hand clamped around his shin, and the other pulled quickly sliding the boot most of the way off his foot. Blinding pain shot through Ford and his back arched, trying to push away from it. Clenching his teeth hard against the glove, he was sure he cracked a couple of them, as he tried unsuccessfully to stop the shout that had been begging to leave his lips. Panting through the pain, a choked cry left his lips as Reef gently tugged the boot the rest of the way off his foot.

He found himself in Reef's arms, his strength and warmth surrounding him as Ford shuddered, the pain and exhaustion overwhelming him. His face pressed against Reef's shoulder, he felt more than heard his soft rumbles of comfort. Fingers gently raked through Ford's hair as he gripped the solid body engulfing him. Soft, four-day old stubble rubbed against his temple as Reef held him close.

"I'm so, so sorry for hurting you."

"S'okay. Not your fault," Ford choked out through his tears, hugging Reef closer.

"I need to take off your pants and then I'll cut your shorts. I'm not putting you through that again." Ford nodded, knowing that the pants would be a lot easier to get off than the boots. "Gonna wrap you in a blanket while I get the fire started too, okay?"

He nodded again, running his hands down Reef's lats to his waist. The muscles contracted at his touch, distracting Ford from the pain still surging through him.

Reef slowly let him lie down again and curled his fingers in the waistband of Ford's pants pulling the material over his hips and down his legs. Warm breath ghosted over his skin as the pants were tugged lower until they were finally off him. Ford's eyes stayed closed as he regulated his breathing, concentrating on each inhale and exhale and enjoying the gentle touches of the man caring for him. The hand slipping under the front of his shorts up his left leg startled Ford. As he opened his eyes, Ford saw Reef's sheepish smile. It had him chuckling. "I don't normally have to bust up my leg to get lucky. I'm usually a lot smoother than this."

"You're lucky having my hand up your shorts. I'm pretty dexterous." Reef laughed. "Actually, being hurt is a sweet deal for you. You'll have some gorgeous nursemaid waiting on your every need. Sponge baths and all. I'm kinda jealous."

"Awww, sweet cheeks, I'll get her to give you one too."

"Thanks, honeybuns," Reef retorted grinning at him, his boyish dimples and warm brown eyes lighting up the room. Warmth curled through Ford's gut. Damn, he was drawn to Reef like honey to a bee. Their gazes collided, the temperature in the air spiking as the chemistry between the two of them sizzled. Neither of them were smiling anymore. Ford was sure his expression mirrored Reef's heated look. His eyes drifted closed, his mouth open a fraction. Ford's sight was drawn down, transfixed on those full lips as Reef licked a trail along the bottom one.

Ford reached out and palmed Reef's cheek, running his thumb along the flesh that he wanted to kiss so much. Ford couldn't explain why. The fact that Reef was a man didn't seem to matter to him in that moment. It all just clicked into place. This man before him was important.

Reef leaned into his caress before pulling back and blinking a few times. "Hold still."

The cold metal of the scissors from Ford's medical pack startled him as Reef touched them to his skin, lining up the shears with his tight shorts. Ford's abs tightened as he stilled, watching Reef quickly cut away the material. The closer he got to his crown jewels, the more freaked out Ford expected to get. Except he wasn't. Reef drew him in and comforted him without even trying.

The scissors were gone quickly, replaced again with those cool fingers skimming across his quivering skin as they curled over the waistband and pulled. Sucking in a breath Ford closed his eyes, and shuddered while Reef pulled down his underwear.

"I'm gonna light the fire. This'll keep you warm until I can get the water heated up for a coffee and a soak, yeah?" Reef murmured close to Ford's ear as he wrapped the foil blanket around his body. Ford was instantly warmer, his breath hissing out as he burrowed down into the sofa curling into the blanket as much as he could with a fucked knee.

BLINKING HIS EYES OPEN, the first thing Ford noticed was the roaring fire. Its warmth had already seeped through the little cabin. Turning toward Reef, he watched in rapt fascination as he bent over. Ford didn't take much notice of what he was doing, just that he was doing it in nothing but those black briefs that hugged his tight ass, leaving the full length of his long muscled legs uncovered. Ford's cock swelled at the sight, going rigid as he imagined pressing up against him. There was no way Ford could deny that he was attracted to Reef. Hell, he couldn't deny it from the first moment they'd spent together. That first night Ford had gripped his dick and stroked himself to an orgasm that nearly blew his mind. The noises that Reef had made settling down to sleep were such a turn on; muffled sighs and gasps. Ford had held onto those sounds and turned them into his own spank bank. He'd erupted like a geyser, blowing in his fist as he fucked into the bed, trying to muffle his shouts of completion by biting down on the pillow. And the second and third night together? Exactly the same result, with stronger ensuing orgasms as he let his imagination wander.

"Hi," Ford croaked.

"Hey, you," Reef responded, coming over to crouch in front of him. "Tub's ready and I have some ice for your knee. Coffee's made and I'm just about to get some dinner for you."

"How long did I sleep for?"

"About half an hour. I've been checking on you though."

"Thanks, Reef. I don't know what I would have done without you today. You're a bloody superhero in my books."

"It was nothing. You would have done the same thing for me." Ford nodded. Truer words were never spoken. The thought of Reef injured or in danger hurt him worse than his own battered up knee.

"Come on, let's get you into the tub. Can you hobble over there or do you need me to carry you?"

"Nah, I can hop." Reef grinned and unwrapped the blanket from around Ford, helping him off the sofa. With his arm wrapped around Reef's shoulders to help support his weight and Reef's around his waist, Ford hopped over to the tub.

"Okay, sit down on the edge and I'll help you get in." Reef stepped into the water and gripped Ford's underarms, balancing him as he twisted and tentatively placed his feet into the water. "I've got your weight, Ford. Just slide in, then I'll get out." Ford did just that, letting his weight rest in Reef's hands.

The world suddenly sped up as Reef let out a surprised sounding yelp, and they crashed into the water. Ford's injured left knee was high up out of the water as he landed on firm muscle and warm skin, water sloshing about them and over the lip of the tub.

"Oh, shit. Shit. Shit. Shit. Are you okay?" Ford could clearly hear the panic in Reef's voice as he struggled to keep them up, all the while sliding around on the slippery surface.

All Ford could do was laugh. Water had splashed everywhere, he was lying on top of a man he was wildly attracted to, and he'd avoided aggravating his hurt knee when they'd fallen. It was the best outcome he could have hoped for. "All good." He laughed again, snuggling side on into Reef's broad chest and enjoying the feel of the strong arms that had come around him.

As Reef pulled himself upright, Ford watched as water rivulets ran down Reef's shoulder over his pecs and down his abs. A single drop hung, perched at the end of Reef's nipple, right in Ford's line of sight. The warm skin beckoned to him, begging him to taste, to tempt, to tease. He leaned toward Reef again, giving into temptation as he reached out with his tongue and licked the tip of Reef's nipple, drinking in the droplet of water. Reef moaned long and low. Ford splayed his hand on Reef's abs massaging his skin as he bent once more toward Reef and swiped a longer, slower lick over his nipple. The saltiness of fresh sweat teased his senses, as Reef took a fistful of his hair and yanked him upward, growling as he stared Ford down. Desire crackled between them, palpable in its intensity. Ford's cock was hard, straining above the waterline, his foreskin pulled back, the glans pulsing with need. Ford wasn't the only one either; Reef's dick was long and thick against his hip. It was such a fucking turn on.

"What the fuck is happening to me?" Reef muttered as his grip in Ford's hair tightened and he moved to smash their mouths together. The door took that moment to crash open, two men in the same black and red ski gear as Ford's busting over the threshold, backboard and medical packs in tow.

"Ford, dude!"

"Lads, hey..." Ford cleared his throat and shook out of the cloud of lust enveloping him. "Ah, you're here."

"Yeah, we got your emergency signal so we came. We were worried that you'd tried to get through the storm at the campsite," Trent, his workmate, said from behind Ricky, the helicopter pilot standing just inside the closed door.

"We detoured here instead. Lads, I need help getting up. I wrecked my knee. Tell me you have a brace I can use." Ford caressed Reef's abs again, the muscle fluttering under his skin.

"I've got one in my pack," Trent replied, as Ricky stopped before the tub.

"We fell in." The excuse may have been the partial truth, but it burned to reduce what had happened between him and Reef to that.

"Sure, dude. You know it's cool if you guys are together. Doesn't make a difference to me," Ricky said softly so that only the three of them could hear.

"Yeah, ah..." Ford hesitated.

"I was trying to help him in – I think he has hypothermia – but I slipped and here we are," Reef explained with a wry grin. Ford watched him speak; he was detached, putting on a façade. But when he turned to Ford looking him in the eyes, that wall fell away and in its place, heat and desire raged.

———

COFFEE. All Reef wanted was good coffee. Hot, strong, freshly roasted decent tasting java. And an

English Breakfast or whatever tea Ford drank; he was too embarrassed to ask when Ford's workmates were around. It wasn't like they were together but damn, the pull between he and Ford was growing stronger. Now, Ford was undergoing scans on his knee to figure out what the damage was. Ford had insisted it wasn't broken and he didn't think it was ligament damage either, but Reef had no idea. Did a muscle tear like that need surgery?

Reef had walked around the small hospital until he'd found the cafeteria tucked away at one end and virtually inhaled his first mug. It was better than the shit at the cabin. Barely. He desperately needed the good stuff, but until he knew what was happening with Ford, he wasn't leaving. He paced the waiting room until a cute nurse came to collect him.

"Ford thought you might still be here. Want to come back and see him?"

"Is he okay?" Reef asked as they walked through the swinging doors of the emergency room.

"See for yourself, hon." The nurse pointed toward a bed with Ford on it. He was dressed in a hospital gown and beanie, with a heavy blanket over him as he stared up at the roof.

"Hey, honeybuns," Reef said softly as he joined Ford at his bedside. "How you holding up?"

"I'm good," he smiled. "Thanks for waiting, but you didn't have to."

"I had no way of contacting you if I left. I never got your number. I thought maybe we could grab a beer. Not now, obviously, but in a few days if you're okay."

"Yeah, I'd like that. I'm stuck in here overnight, but when I get out we'll go."

"Is it that bad?"

"No, it's exactly what I thought, just a torn muscle. I'll be in a brace to keep it immobile for a week or so and physio after that. The bruises are all to be expected too, there's no damage to my ribs or my hip, but they're keeping me in overnight to be cautious. Apparently they're a little freaked that you pulled me out of an avalanche a few hours ago." Ford grinned.

"*I'm* a little freaked out that I pulled you out of an avalanche a few hours ago! Shit, you coulda died."

"I'll be out of action for a few weeks, but it could have been so much worse. I'm feelin' pretty lucky right about now."

"Lotto ticket, dude." Reef squeezed Ford's forearm and smiled. "Hey, you had that cup of tea you were after yet?"

"Urgh, yes. It was almost as bad as the coffee."

"Yeah, my coffee was pretty bad, too."

"Hi Ford," a doctor in aqua-colored scrubs and a

white lab coat said from the edge of the curtained off area. "I need to check your vitals."

"I'll give you some privacy. I'll be back in half hour or so with that tea you were after, okay?"

"Thank you." Ford smiled and Reef's heart warmed. This man... he was something special. Stepping away from the bed, Ford snagged his hand squeezing his fingers. "I'll tell the desk to let you know where I am."

"See you soon." It took all his strength not to lean down and kiss him. Instead Reef squeezed Ford's fingers in return and backed out of the room, not breaking their gaze until he reached the swinging doors to exit the emergency department.

TWENTY-FOUR HOURS LATER

"I COULD HAVE MET you in the bar. You didn't have to come all the way out here to pick me up, Reef."

"It's only a five minute drive out of town."

"Urgh, I feel like an invalid. I hate not being able to drive." Ford's frustration was evident already, especially as he struggled with his boots.

"It's only temporary. Don't be a baby." Reef smiled, dropping to his knees and doing up the laces on the Doc Martins before tugging his dark blue boot leg jeans over the top. From this angle, Ford's legs looked longer and even with the brace around his knee, stronger. His chest and shoulders were broad, begging Reef to touch every inch of the black button down shirt and caress everything under it. He was damn sexy.

Standing, Reef ran his fingers through Ford's perfectly mussed up curls, messing them even more, "Now come on, up. Let's get this beer."

"Don't mess the do, dude! These curls get the girls." Ford flashed him a grin full of heat and promise but Reef's gut twisted. When he'd returned to the hospital with a box of tea leaves for Ford, things got a little weird. Reef didn't know what to do with the feelings he had. He was trying to get back that easy friendship they had in the cabin, but something wasn't right. Was all this emotional upheaval caused by them being stuck together? Had the attraction fired simply because of adrenaline? They'd survived two life-threatening situations together. Maybe that had screwed around with his equilibrium and he didn't really feel the way he felt. Yeah, it sounded ridiculous even to Reef's own mind.

"Fuck off, idiot." Reef pasted on a smile trying to put on a brave face, but Ford saw straight through it.

"Hey, what's wrong?" Ford asked as he gripped Reef's biceps squeezing them gently.

"Nothing. S'all good. Let's do this."

REEF PARALLEL PARKED the SUV Momma Bear had booked for him in the on-street park a few doors down from the bar Ford had directed him to. It wasn't much to look at from street level, just a doorway with a backlit sign proclaiming it was 'The London', and a set of stairs leading down to the basement club. Reef hesitated only for a moment until he saw Ford tackling the stairs like a pro. Like any skier or snowboarder, he'd been on crutches a few times before.

Inside the club was vibin'. There were a bunch of tables set up overlooking the open kitchen, and a little beyond that, a bar and dance floor. The restaurant was near full, every seat along the bar occupied and a handful of people already dancing to the music pulsing through the sound system.

"Let's get some food first." Ford motioned with his head as he hobbled over to a free booth using his crutches. Reef slid in opposite him.

"What's good?"

"Everything. These sampler plates are the way to go. You've got to try the brisket and this chicken. Oh, and this salad. And the flatbread."

"Why don't you order for both of us, and I'll get the drinks?"

"Sure."

Reef headed over to the bar and ordered the ciders for him and Ford. Lost in his thoughts, he didn't see the two girls who'd joined Ford at the table until he was almost on top of them. Ford laughed at something the pretty blonde one said and jealousy speared through him as her arm snaked around Ford's, hugging his thick bicep to her body. Reef wasn't an envious guy. He wasn't possessive. He wasn't one of those alpha assholes who had to piss on everything and beat their chests to mark their territory.

Ordinarily.

Tonight? He was in unchartered territory. It was supposed to be his and Ford's night. He wanted it to be just the two of them, awkwardness be damned. And now they had two cute girls joining them.

Reef almost slapped himself across the back of the head. They had two cute girls sitting at their booth. One was clearly coming onto Ford and the other one, a curvy brunette with long curls, had turned and was watching his approach. Hip black glasses framed her pretty eyes and bright pink lipstick gave her a not-so-sweet-and-innocent air. Her hair was swept to the side showing every inch of creamy skin on her back, revealed by a top that was barely more than a scrap of material held together with straps crisscrossing over her.

"Ladies," Reef smiled. He was not going to be a dick about the ladies crashing their... date.

Even if it killed him.

The smile must have looked more like a cringe; Ford's eyebrows hiked up and he regarded him for a moment before introducing the girls. The one who'd apparently set her sights on Reef was Shelly. She and Ford were work friends.

Reef's mood soured even more as their food arrived with two extra plates and everyone looked to him to buy another round of drinks. He was kinda glad that he had the excuse to leave the table. Whatsher-name was flirting shamelessly with Ford, and Ford didn't exactly hate it. Shelly had backed off a little, people watching instead of flirting with him. It wasn't like he didn't want the attention, it was just coming from the wrong person. Urgh. He sounded like a fucking sap.

Standing up at the bar, Reef ordered another two ciders and glasses of red for the girls. While he was waiting, an arm snaked around his waist and floral perfume teased his nose.

"So," Shelly said from beside him.

"So," Reef responded, forcing a grin at her.

"Need some help?"

"No, I've got this. You go have fun." Reef cringed. Shit, he'd let his big mouth run, and revealed too much.

"You aren't having fun?"

"It's not that. I haven't known Ford for long. I was kinda expecting we'd have a few drinks and hang out. And now I sound like a girl."

"Hey, there's nothing wrong with being a girl." Shelly playfully punched him, her other arm never leaving his waist. "Look, I'm sorry we crashed your party. I can see you aren't interested in a one night hook-up and I'm glad about that. Maybe the two of us can get together again when you and Ford aren't having a bro-date."

"Um, yeah. Maybe."

"Good, now let's get these drinks back to the thirsty masses."

"Sure." He nodded, placating her. Shelly was exactly his type – long brown curly hair, perfect skin and teeth, pouty lips that he could almost imagine kissing. Almost. Instead he kept imagining much shorter brown curly hair, striking eyes that were the bluest of blue, a day or two of stubble, broad shoulders and strong arms. All he wanted was to have some fun hanging out with Ford by themselves. Jesus, he sounded like a whiny jealous bitch. What was wrong with him? Running his fingers through his hair, Reef let out a slow breath and shook his head.

THE REST of the night was a disaster. Shelly had wanted to dance so Reef danced. Kate wanted to move over to the bar so they had done that even though it was uncomfortable for Ford. And because the place was hoppin', they'd only managed to snag two chairs. Ford was sitting with Kate standing between his outstretched legs and her arms around his shoulders, while Shelly took the other seat. And Reef sulked, leaning up against the bar drinking sodas so he didn't do anything stupid and declare how hot he was for Ford in a humiliating drunken rant.

"Ladies, I've had fun, but I'm in need of some painkillers and bed."

"I'm glad you're okay, Ford. We were worried the whole time you guys were out on the mountain."

"Can't say that I'd be here without Reef. He's a fucking superhero."

"Here, here." Shelly toasted as she raised her glass.

Reef watched Kate put the move on Ford. Her eyes dropped to his mouth and hers opened and she leaned into him and ran her fingers through the curls at the base of Ford's neck. Jealousy flared hot and fast like a California wildfire ripping through Reef. Clenching his fists and jaw, he turned. He couldn't watch Ford kiss her.

"Nice meeting you, Reef. Call me at the heli-ski center if you want to catch up again."

"That's where I know you from? Shit, sorry Shelly. I didn't even put two and two together."

"No, I can see why though." Shelly gave him a small smile and squeezed his arm. "Go on and take Ford home. He needs you."

It was slow getting out of the club – Ford being on crutches made it difficult to steer through the mass of people in there, and just as slow walking back to Reef's rental. They were silent as they made their way to the SUV.

Unlocking the doors, Reef opened the passenger side and stepped aside so Ford could get in. Instead, of doing that, Ford leaned his ass against the SUV. "What's going on? You've been in a bloody pissy mood since we left my house."

"I'm fine, nothing's wrong." Reef lied. Shit, how many times had Addilyn said the same thing to him when he'd called? He'd never understood how wrong things actually were when that phrase was uttered, until now.

"C'mere," Ford murmured, tugging on Reef's blazer. "There *is* something wrong. You've never been like this before—"

"What, in the four days we've known each other?" Reef snapped sarcastically. Ford didn't respond, instead yanking hard on Reef's jacket until he staggered toward him. They were standing toe to toe, both in black boots, both in blue jeans, both with black leather belts. Ford's black button down was paired with a black jacket, whilst Reef's black blazer was worn over the top of a tight white thermal shirt. None of that mattered though, as Reef stared into those amazing blue eyes. The chemistry sparked between them and exploded when Ford dropped his heated gaze down to Reef's mouth. They moved simultaneously, Ford pushing his crutches away so they clattered to the ground and reached out, one hand on Reef's waist and the other grasping the back of his neck. Reef's hands went straight into Ford's hair, spearing through the curls. They were breathing hard, their bodies pressed against each other. Reef held Ford's head still, stopping him from crashing their mouths together.

"She touched your fucking hair," Reef ground out.

"I want your hands there, not he—" Reef's mouth covered Ford's, drowning the words on a moan. Firm but soft lips pressed against his, his own opening immediately as Reef's tongue licked the seam. Their tongues dueled in a kiss so hot that they could have spontaneously combusted.

It was fire.

Passion.

Need.

Strong arms held Reef close, wrapping him in an embrace that he melted into. Muscled chest pressed against muscled chest, Ford's cock, a steely length, pressed next to his own. Reef couldn't get close enough. He leaned on Ford pushing him harder against the back door of the rental, grinding against him as a rumbling moan sounded between them. Reef had no idea whether it was he or Ford who made the noise, it was so full of desire it was almost painful. Tearing his mouth from Ford's he pulled back, but Ford didn't let him move away. Those powerful arms pinned him against Ford's body as Reef fingered those curls he'd become obsessed with.

"Don't pull back. Don't regret this," Ford whispered.

"I don't. It feels too right. Jesus, I know how girls get crazy psycho jealous now."

"I'm sorry, I tried not to encourage Kate, but she wouldn't take the hint." Reef furrowed his brows thinking back. He'd been so caught up with Kate's hands all over Ford that he hadn't taken any notice of what Ford was doing in return. When they were sitting in the booth, Ford sat directly opposite Reef. His arms were down by his sides. Kate's arm was hooked through his. When they were sitting at the bar, Ford had sat down, propping his left leg on the other stool they had snagged. Kate had angled herself between his legs and wrapped her arms around his shoulders. Ford hadn't hugged her back. In fact, he hadn't touched her the whole night except a hand on her arm when he kissed her on the cheek as they were leaving.

"You kissed her," Reef murmured, as he leaned forward, pressing his lips to Ford's again. "I. Wanted. To. Do. That," he whispered, kissing Ford between each word.

Ford pulled back. "Shelly hugged you. I wanted to do that." Ford tightened his grip around Reef's waist and tugged him closer. Every inch of their bodies were pressed against each other. Reef's breath hitched as their lips met and melded in a slower kiss. Soft stubble stroked Reef's lips as he kissed a line down Ford's jaw to his throat before sucking in his lobe, and working his way back to those lips that were too tempting to turn away from. Tongues gently touching, Reef explored Ford's mouth in unhurried swipes, licking and playfully flicking against the other. Letting Ford's hair go, he ran his right hand down Ford's sculpted chest and abs, missing the bruises caused by the avalanche. Reef kept his touch gentle, pulling away the instant a hiss left Ford's lips.

"Don't stop. I love your hands on me. I couldn't get enough of touching you when we were in that bloody cabin." Reef hummed his agreement as his hand lowered back to Ford's bruised side and connected their mouths again, slowly kissing him.

The "Get a room, homos," shouted from a passing car barely registered until another shout of, "fucking fags," was yelled with a thick accent.

"Is that us they're talking about?" Ford asked. Reef couldn't help but laugh.

"I suppose it is. Come on, I'll get you home."

"Will you stay?"

"I don't know if I'm ready for us to go further, Ford."

"I know. I'm not either, but I'd really like to pash you again."

"Okay. I can do that." Reef grinned, a matching smile spreading across Ford's face.

CHAPTER SIX

FORD COULDN'T KEEP his eyes off the gorgeous man in front of him. Reef's gaze was glued to the road, only looking back at Ford for the briefest of seconds. He noticed the shy smiles Reef was trying to contain and they made him smile too. Right at that moment, Ford loved being the passenger. He could openly stare at Reef and he took every opportunity to do just that. Only a frown line on his forehead marred his damn near perfect profile. Reef's knuckles were clenched tight on the steering wheel; he looked like he was ready to pounce. For someone so laid back, it was strange seeing him like that. Ford's best guess was that driving on the left hand side of the road was stressing Reef out. He laughed, picturing Reef repeating a set of mental instructions to himself – *drive on the left side of the road, give way to oncoming traffic turning right, drive clockwise through roundabouts.* They were the same instructions Ford ran through when he returned from Italy every year.

"What?" Reef asked when Ford laughed again, this time at Reef's self-satisfied grin as he managed a roundabout.

"Pretty happy with yourself, huh?"

"This shit is hard. I've never driven on this side of the road before."

"You're doing well."

"You sound like Coach when he was teaching me to drive. *Well done, son,*" Reef repeated in a deep drawl. *"Now keep your speed down and watch out for grannies and babes.* I though he meant cute girls until I pointed out one to him and said 'there's a babe.' Needless to say, that wasn't what he was talking about." Ford couldn't help but laugh again. Reef was lucky he'd found Momma Bear and Coach. He wished he'd had that sort of influence while growing up. His father had been all about Ford getting the best grades possible so he could graduate with honors, and continue the family legacy of being a surgeon. He'd had his whole life mapped out for him, starting with Ford going to the same medical school his father had attended, and ending with the same surgical specialization. Ford's act of defiance – withdrawing the application his father had so meticulously filled out – hadn't won any favors with his old man. Looking back, Ford's little plan of quietly going to that university's biggest competitor was doomed to fail. His father had been livid when no acceptance letter arrived. He'd called up the Vice-Chancellor of the university, who of course he had on speed dial as they'd graduated together, only to find out that Ford's application hadn't been processed. Between the two of them, a House of Lords inquiry was almost ordered until they found a record of Ford's letter. As long as he was an honor-roll student his father never cared enough to get involved much in his life, but Ford copped a beat down that day.

Having someone like Momma Bear and Coach? That would have been nice.

"You okay?" Reef's hand landed on his right knee, squeezing lightly. "You were in your own little world."

Ford gave him a small smile. "I'm okay now that I'm here with you."

"Aww, so sweet, honeybuns." Reef's grin instantly eased the bad memories of that chapter in his life and made him ache to have him in his arms again. It wasn't just sexual either. Reef grounded him in a way that he'd never experienced before. Ford was waiting for his attraction to Reef to get weird, to let the 'gay' thing freak him out. But it just wasn't happening.

His seatbelt was unbuckled before they'd even come to a complete stop and the door thrown open while Reef was still shutting off the ignition. "Keen to get inside are you?" Reef asked playfully.

"Is that a problem?" Ford hiked his eyebrow up as he looked at Reef questioningly. His man just laughed and hopped out, pulling Ford's crutches off the back seat.

"Come in," Ford said as he hobbled into the laundry room off his kitchen.

"Sit down. I'll help you with your boots." Reef leaned into Ford and squeezed his biceps gently.

"I hate this. I hate not being able to do such basic things."

"Hush. Let me look after you." Cupping his cheek, Reef brushed his lips over Ford's. Blowing out the deep breath he held, Reef asked, "You sure about this, Ford? This is a big step. I'm kinda freakin' out."

"Because I'm a man? Never mind, that's a stupid question." Ford took a moment to think about how to frame his thoughts. "Normally I jump into bed with any girl I fancy. I'm never worried about the day after because she knows I won't be there. With you it's different. I'm wildly attracted to you and I like you too.

I'm not gonna lie, if I sit here and think on it for too long I'll probably freak myself out. But I want to get to know you better. I was planning on taking a page outta your book and going with the flow."

"What happens if we have regrets tomorrow?"

"Then we talk about it and get through it, whatever we decide."

"Yeah?"

"Yeah, sweet cheeks, that's exactly what we do." Ford let the crutch fall against the wall and wrapped his arm around Reef's waist, pulling him close as Reef's smile lit up the room again. "But I'd really like not to have regrets."

Reef hummed, agreeing as Ford brought their mouths together again kissing him slowly, their tongues caressing, exploring each other. Reef's lips were firm against his as Ford deepened the kiss. Ford kissed his way to Reef's throat and licked his pulse point as Reef threaded his fingers into Ford's hair, gently tugging at the curls. Hearing Reef's breath catch was the sexiest thing. At least that was until Reef growled low in his throat. If there was any doubt before that Ford's cock was hard, there wasn't anymore. He could hammer nails with it. Reef's big body, his aftershave – something spicy and fresh – his strength, his stubble. God, what it did to Ford.

Hair prickled his cheek as Ford kissed his way back to Reef's mouth. One hand left Ford's hair, Reef's grasp firm as he kneaded the muscles in Ford's shoulders all the way to the small of his back. Shudders rocked through Ford. Women were beautiful, amazing, gorgeous, but Reef? He instinctively knew how to touch him. *Where* to touch. His hair, the junction between his Trapezius and Latissimus Dorsi muscles in the middle of his back. Both hot buttons. Both pressed with such easy skill and finesse that he had Ford grinding his hips against him seeking relief. He didn't hesitate working the spots, pressing and tugging as his tongue delved deep.

The sound of the other crutch clattering to the floor startled them apart. Gasping in much needed oxygen, Reef panted in his ear, "Boots, Ford. Then clothes. Want you." Reef's warm breath washed against Ford's throat as he spoke, sending sparks of need through him.

"Take it slow," Ford murmured. "Remember, no regrets tomorrow."

"Hmmm," Reef moaned against Ford's throat. "Sit. Before I strip you right here."

Ford sat in the nearby chair as Reef unlaced and tugged off his right boot.

"Socks off?"

"Please," Ford murmured as he ran a hand through his own hair trying to get his body under control. Reef on his knees before him conjured up images of them naked together while Reef used those skilled hands and tongue on other parts of his anatomy. Ford knew it was too soon for that, but he hoped it was a possibility. The thought of touching Reef too and exploring his perfect body was just as tempting.

"Lift up a little, Ford." Reef guided, touching his left leg. Ford obliged and Reef's snort of laughter had him chuckling too. "How have you managed to wear boots all night without a sock on?"

"Wasn't exactly comfortable, but I couldn't get it on."

"You could have asked for help."

"I told you I hate feelin' like an invalid." Ford shrugged, a little embarrassed at himself.

"You're damn stubborn. You know that?"

"Been told a time or two." Ford smiled at Reef's grin. "Come on, let me give you a tour of Casa Wallace." Ford hobbled through the doorway into the combined open plan kitchen, living and dining rooms. He was proud of his design efforts. He'd styled his little cottage like a loft apartment. Exposed bricks, high ceilings and heavy roof beams created an industrial vibe while the polished hardwood floors, feature fireplace, rugs and cushy furniture gave the place warmth. Giant floor to ceiling windows – now covered by the closed drapes – ran along one entire side of the house. The vista during the day was spectacular. The black window frames bracketed a view of both the Remarkables Range that his house sat at the foot of, and Queenstown proper. On a near full moon like tonight, the outline of the mountains would still be clearly visible, the behemoth lying like a quiet sentinel above them.

"Bathroom's through there. Let me light the fire and I'll show you the bedroom. Office is at the other end of the house."

"Ford." Reef stilled him. "Let me do the fire. I'll bring you a drink and some painkillers while you go lie down. Just tell me what you need."

"I don't need painkillers. It was just an excuse to get out of there. But if you could light the fire, that'd be great. Pain in the ass to get down onto the floor." Reef squeezed his arm affectionately and patted Ford on the ass as he grinned.

Ford hobbled into the bedroom and was grateful that he was in there a couple of minutes before Reef. He hadn't had the chance to tidy up before they'd left. There were clothes strewn about the place from trying on three different pairs of trousers and jeans, before finally settling on the fourth pair. Choosing a shirt had taken him longer. Seven discarded ones decorated his bedroom floor. Ford rehung each of the shirts and stuffed the jeans back onto the shelves in his closet. He straightened the dark grey and taupe duvet and plumped up the pillows resting against the heavy timber frame. Happy with the state of the room, he turned the bedside lamp on low before flicking off the overhead light. Pulling the drapes in the bedroom closed was the final thing Ford did before sitting down on the edge of the bed.

"Nice place, Ford," Reef commented from the doorway.

"Why you standing all the way over there?"

"You ever done this before? Been with a man? Even been attracted to a man?"

"No." He paused. "But something hasn't exactly been right, either. You'd think by the time a man is thirty-three years old he'd have wanted to settle down or at least dated *one* of the ladies he'd been with. But nope. The closest thing to a long-term relationship I've had, is dating for six months. And we weren't exclusive for most of that. Why didn't I want something more?"

"So, you think you're in the closet?"

"I think it's more that I haven't found the right

person. I haven't wanted to try. You make me reconsider things."

"You scared of what it means?"

Ford thought on that for a moment. "No, I'm not
scared." He shook his head slowly. "I don't give a rats
what anyone thinks of me. I've lived with my father's
disappointment all my life. Whatever I do will never
be enough for him, so I don't even try to please him or
anyone else anymore. Strangers' opinions mean nothing. My friends - well the good ones, anyway - won't
give a shit who I'm shagging either."

Reef's hands were in his pockets, his shoulders
hunched. Looking down at the floor, he mumbled, "I'm
worried about Coach's reaction. I don't want to disap-
point him. He's given me so much. I think Momma
Bear will be happy as long as I am, but I'm not sure.
What happens if they don't want to have anything to
do with me anymore? I'll lose them. That scares me."

"Come here, sit down." Reef nodded and shrugged
off his jacket draping it over the chair in the corner of
the room before sitting stiffly on the bed.

"Have you been with a man before, Reef?"

"No." Reef shook his head and cracked every one
of his knuckles, all the while not meeting Ford's gaze.

"But you've been attracted to men."

A breath whooshed out of Reef's lungs. "Yeah, once. He was my mentor on the pro-circuit."

Ford got a sinking feeling. Reef was anxious. Gone was the glimpse of passion he'd seen. In its place was discomfort and... something else he couldn't identify. He needed to know. "What happened between you two?"

"Nothing. He had a girl back home and retired a few years after I started on the pro-circuit. We email each other every now and then, but nothing else." Ford let out a relieved breath. He despised the idea of Reef being with another man. It wasn't like being with a woman; they'd both done that, but the thought of another man's hands on him rubbed Ford the wrong way. *Mine* kept ringing through his head.

"Do you still like him?"

"No. It's been a long time since I felt anything for him." Ford shifted on the bed so he and Reef were facing each other. Threading their fingers together, Ford squeezed them. Reef still didn't look at him and physically pulled away. Ford could almost see Reef's resolve waver. He was leaving.

Desperate to stop that from happening, Ford said the first thing that popped into his head. "Let's keep this between us. We'll have some fun, keep it casual. It's not like we have to get serious." Ford shrugged trying to come off as nonchalant. "We don't have to tell anyone." A sick feeling fell over him. That's not what he wanted. The truth of it was that Reef was the first person he actually wanted more with. But how could he lay it all out there again, expose himself that much only to have his heart torn to shreds when Reef walked away? Ford understood; losing your family sucked. When his father had stopped speaking to him, Ford's mother had followed suit, callus bitch that she was. Ford got the hugely generous secret thirty-second call on his birthday and at Christmas as a result. That sucked, but Reef spoke to Momma Bear and Coach a few times a week – more than Ford had spoken with his parents, perhaps ever. Ford would be shattered if Reef's relationship with his pseudo-parents degenerated into that. Coach and Momma Bear were really the only two people Reef had in the world. His real parents were so flaky, they were really nothing more than DNA-donors and like Ford, Reef was an only child. There wasn't any other family he was close to either. That left Ford as the disposable one in Reef's circle. And didn't that thought sting.

———

REEF MET Ford's gaze with a little prompting from

Ford's fingers under his chin, forcing his face up. The emotion he saw in Ford's eyes belied his flippant remark. At least that's what Reef was hoping for. Was it a pipedream that a man who did nothing but casual hook-ups might actually feel something more for him? Probably. Was Reef's heart going to shatter when Ford walked away? Absolutely. Reef may have been uncertain about how to deal with his family and scared of their reaction, but he knew himself well enough to recognize he was crushing on Ford. Hard. Were any of the worries going to stop him? Not in a million years. He leaned forward and brushed his lips against Ford's, closing his eyes as he gripped the button down shirt that molded to every muscle in Ford's bulkier body, pulling him closer.

They tumbled to the bed, their bodies communicating in a language far more meaningful than the words spoken between them. Their lips melding together and tongues stroking, Reef slipped his hands under Ford's shirt, running his fingertips over the planes and valleys of his toned body. Ford's heart raced under Reef's palm as Reef pressed him into the sheets, the bulk beneath his body the perfect size.

Ford's stubble was soft against Reef's mouth. He mapped Ford's throat, kissing, nibbling and licking every inch of skin that he could reach. Encouraged by

Ford's moans and the strong hands squeezing Reef's shoulders, Reef flicked open the buttons on Ford's shirt one by one, revealing a few extra inches of skin with each and a dusting of dark hair over his chest. He wasn't trying to tease Ford, but the man's skin was irresistible. Smooth, pale, it begged to be tasted. Reef worshiped Ford's body as he moaned and writhed below him.

"Jesus you're sexy, Ford. Every inch of your skin is flawless. I can see every muscle, feel every one of them quiver when I kiss you."

Ford moaned, apparently unable to form a coherent response anymore. Reef slowed, losing himself in the moment. Breathing in his scent, loving the warm, smooth skin of Ford's abs, Reef ran his nose down Ford's happy trail to his belt before licking along the valley between his abs then up and around Ford's navel. Ford tensed, a shudder ripping through him as he fisted the sheets, a desperate sounding cry leaving his lips. Reef instantly missed the firm grip on his shoulder, helping him read the language Ford's body was speaking. Every squeeze, every tremble encouraging him to keep going. Ford palmed his dick, thrusting the hard shaft into his firm grip. Reef's own cock was as hard as a fence paling, begging to be released from the tight confines of his jeans. Visions of their naked bodies writhing against each other, bare skin moving together, passionate kisses and the strength of their touches sent a pulse of need through Reef's body. He wanted this man. More than he'd ever wanted anything before.

"Fuck," Ford moaned. The want in his voice had Reef breathing out on a ragged exhale.

"I want you, Ford. I wanna get naked with you and love on every part of you. I wanna make you shout my name."

"Close now," Ford panted. "Feel so good on me, Reef. But I wanna touch you too. Get naked."

Reef hummed against his skin, the vibrations seemingly affecting Ford as much as Reef's licking and nibbling had. Slowly trailing his lips up to his exposed nipples, Reef swirled his tongue around the pebbled points making Ford's breath hitch, his soft bite eliciting a moan. He loved that Ford was so responsive, every movement against his skin caused a reaction, fueling Reef's lust into a fire. He knew that even though Ford hooked up regularly, it'd been a long time since he'd been shown some lovin' himself – Ford admitted as much when they were in the ranger's cabin – but he hadn't expected the passion between them to have the explosive power it did. Every tense, every breath, every sound from Ford left Reef in no doubt that he was on the steady climb towards one hell of an orgasm. And Reef so desperately wanted to take him there, to be the one who could give him that. He caressed his way up Ford's jaw, hovering over him as he straddled his legs. Reef's world had turned upside down in the last few hours. Well, days really. Since he'd noticed Ford, he'd opened the door on his sexuality, something he thought he'd closed off a long time ago. And Reef was good with that, comfortable. Finally, he felt like he fit in his own skin, like he could be who he truly was without holding back, without hiding. He craved a rough touch, a strong hand to pin him down, but he needed to be able to do the same. The women in Reef's life had all been so tiny that he could've snapped them in two, but Ford? He could handle it, he could give it. And damn, the man writhing below him was something else, hot as hell.

"Kiss me, Reef," Ford whispered, as his big hands cupped Reef's shoulder and the back of his neck, bringing Reef down to him again. Their mouths slammed together, ferocious need consuming him. Instinct took over, their bodies rocking and rolling against the other's. Solid muscles between Reef's spread thighs, hardness under his palms, firm lips and a strong tongue against his, a cock straining equally as hard as Reef's against the denim constricting it.

Clamping his teeth down, Reef bit Ford's bottom lip and thrust hard, grinding their hips together, rutting breathlessly against each other. The sound of Ford's moan went straight to his cock.

Ford slipped his hands between their bodies to undo his belt. His desperation was palpable; Reef was at the same point. Tearing his mouth away from Ford's, Reef let his eyes wander down the body of the gorgeous man below him. Ripping open his jeans, Ford pushed them down off his hips, letting them pool under his ass. Panting, he copied Ford's move, kicking his jeans off altogether. Ford watched him like a hawk, his tongue licking along his bottom lip before his teeth sunk into the kiss-swollen flesh. It'd been a long time since Reef felt sexy, had that confidence coursing through his veins that only the unbridled lust of another person could bring to the fore and he used every ounce of it to pull Ford's jeans and underwear down his legs. The bruises on Ford's hip and ribs were still pronounced, but healing quickly. His knee was still horribly swollen, so as much as Reef craved a rough touch, he was gentle, cautious.

Both naked, with Reef kneeling at Ford's outstretched legs, he paused. This was a whole new ball game. Making out was one thing. Touching each other's naked bodies was quite another. Was Reef ready for this? Was he ready to cross that final bridge to recognize who he truly was? With this man – hell yes. He grinned, his dimples no doubt showing as his smile widened seeing Ford's reaction. The lust and affection in his stare floored Reef. Had anyone ever looked at him like that before?

Ford sat up, doing an effortless crunch that had every one of his muscles rippling and Reef almost swallowing his tongue. Damn. He was speechless. Lust ripped through him, overtaking him with frenzied need. He was gonna lose his mind if Ford pulled back now.

"Reef," Ford murmured. "I want you." His hands outstretched, Ford beckoned to him. Those words, his actions washed over Reef. Closing his eyes he savored the moment, the knowledge that he was wanted as much as Reef desired him. He couldn't stand the distance between them anymore. Giving into his body's demands he pounced, climbing over the top of Ford, twining their fingers together and pushing Ford's hands above his head. Forcing him down onto the mattress, Reef took his lips in a demanding kiss, thrusting his tongue into Ford's open mouth. The moan Ford let loose had Reef's cock pulsing. Bodies pressed together they rocked into each other, the friction and pre-cum creating a warm wet glove that surrounded him. Tongues dancing, Reef pinned Ford to the bed, thrusting his hips again.

Hard cock sliding on hard cock.

Muscled abs pressed against muscled abs.

Legs tightly wrapped around hips.

Reef's body was in overload. Every sensation was like lightening sparking an inferno. Ford pulling his hands from Reef's grip caused him to moan; a shard of lust ripping through his body at the knowledge that Ford was strong enough to fight back. Caveman reasoning or not, the thought of overpowering Ford or being pinned by him was fucking hot.

Ford wrapped his arm around Reef's waist pulling him tighter against his hips, the other gripping his shoulders, melding every inch of their bodies together. "Oh, fuck," Reef moaned. His hips pumped a stilted tattoo, grinding, rolling, rocking as the tingle at the base of his spine grew. "So close," he whimpered.

"Gonna come," Ford ground out as his rhythm faltered too.

"Kiss me, Ford," he murmured, Ford's eyes fluttering open at the request. Reef was sure his expression held all the crazy emotions running through him – lust, desire, affection and something more. Reef had fallen hard for him. He wanted to tell Ford how much he liked him, how much he meant to him, but the words got caught in the lump in his throat. Instead, their lips met, surprisingly slow and gentle compared to their other kisses. Tongues connected, caressed, loved on each other. The orgasm that blew through Reef surprised him with its speed, but not its strength. One minute he was close, the next he was jetting out ribbon after ribbon of cum from his throbbing dick, shouting as he pitched over the edge into ecstasy. A fireworks show lit behind his closed eyelids as his orgasm roared through him. His body arched and bowed, trembled and quaked through the climax as Ford called his name in a strangled moan, his own cum joining Reef's on their bellies as he pumped his hips again and again.

Breathless, Reef dropped his weight onto Ford. Usually he had enough presence of mind to roll to the side.

Not this time.

It was a revolution. A coup. He was a changed man. Being with a woman had been special, but this? This was life altering. This was everything. Surely his family couldn't fault him for this, not when it was so perfect, not when they had such a crazy connection. Could they?

Nuzzling his face into Ford's neck, Reef basked in the tight embrace Ford wrapped him in. Soft open-mouthed kisses pressed along Reef's throat as Ford finger-combed his hair. Reef breathed him in deeply, running his fingertips down Ford's pecs and back up to the nape of his neck. They laid there together, a sticky mess, not wanting to let go.

"I need to clean you up," Ford murmured.

"Mmhmm."

"Let go and I'll grab us something." Reef planted a kiss on Ford's collarbone and loosened his hold as Ford slipped away, using a single crutch to help him hobble out the door to the bedroom. Momentarily back with a warm washcloth, he wiped it over Reef and tossed it aside before climbing back in to spoon him, pulling the covers over them.

"You like looking after people, don't you?" Reef murmured, his eyes closed.

"I like looking after you," he responded, wrapping his arm around Reef's waist.

Turning his head, Reef murmured, "Kiss me again, then." Their lips met and melded, caressing each other slowly, lazily. Reef hummed and Ford squeezed him tighter, pressing every inch of their bodies together. Breaking apart after more lazy, open-mouthed kisses, they snuggled down into the covers. Reef's eyes closed and he drifted, completely sated. Peaceful. Yeah, that was it; peaceful.

CHAPTER SEVEN

FORD WAS WIDE AWAKE. It wasn't very often that he actually slept with another person in the bed. He wasn't proud of the fact that he tended to disappear before morning even if his partners knew it was a no-strings affair. But Reef's warm body wasn't the problem. No, Ford was the one wrapped around Reef not the other way around. His skin was smooth under Ford's palm and Reef sighed as Ford trailed a line of kisses along his shoulder up his throat. Burying his nose in Reef's hair he inhaled, smelling something spicy rather than fruity. That's when things got weird for Ford. What was he doing lying in bed with a man? A very naked man. A downright sexy sonofabitch too. Their time together the night before, had been a crazy explosion of chemistry. Ford hadn't intended to get naked with him and get off, but neither of them could stop. It wasn't that he had regrets, but... well, maybe he did. Not about Reef, never him.

He crawled out of bed, tucking the covers tight around Reef so he wouldn't stir. Everything could be fixed with a cup of tea – or maybe a scotch – and he needed to think. What if Reef's family gave him an ultimatum? Or worse, told him they never wanted to see him again? Coach and Momma Bear meant the world to Reef. Could Ford handle being the cause if Reef lost them? What about his own family? Ford had a great circle of friends who he was sure would be there for him no matter what, but he ached to have a better relationship with his parents despite what he'd told Reef. Could he risk losing them all over again? Pulling on the same jeans he wore the night before, he hopped over to his crutches and hobbled out of the room, shutting the door behind him quietly.

As the tea was steeping Ford randomly jiggled the bag, staring at the color change. He was lost in thought when a bird chirped outside the window. He looked up, the morning sunshine beckoning to him. Moving over to the large windows on one crutch, he drew the drapes across to let the light inside. Taking his mug to sit in the sun was messy, but not too bad; by the time he slumped down onto the chair he still had three-quarters of it left. Ford closed his eyes, letting his head fall back and the winter sun warm him. His mind ran rampant, every possible scenario flashing through it. His thoughts turned decidedly depressing. How could they possibly make something between them work? Did he even want that? But how could he walk away from Reef? There was no way he could say goodbye. Maybe friends with benefits? No, that didn't sound right either. It had hurt Ford when he'd suggested keeping it casual. He was way more invested in this than he'd realized. There was no hope of protecting his heart when whatever they had turned to shit. And he had to be realistic, it *would* turn to shit.

Ford sighed. "Grow the fuck up, man. You want Reef. You wanna fuck him and you want to be with him. No running. No regrets." Hearing the words out loud solidified everything, laid all his doubt to rest. He smiled. All the uncertainty, all the what-ifs didn't matter. They could make it work. They *would* make it work. He didn't need to be sitting out there in the kitchen anymore. He was going back to bed to his man. Huh, his man. That sounded bloody good.

A bashing on the front door had him lifting himself out of the chair and moving toward it. Turning the lock, he pulled open the heavy timber door. "Trent, hey."

"Dude! Brought over some breakfast burritos to heat up. Figured you'd be starvin' yourself if you can't cook," he said, pushing past Ford into the living room.

"Thanks. I, ah, don't want to sound ungrateful but now isn't a good time."

"Pity sex, nice. Who'd you score with?"

"You're a pig."

"Woah, dude. What's he doing walkin' around naked in your house?" Ford spun around to see Reef wearing absolutely nothing, staggering toward the bathroom. His hair stood on end, his eyes virtually closed as he rubbed his face. On hearing Trent's voice he finally looked up, his eyes widening. Ford's heart leaped into his throat. The man was gorgeous, a gorgeous half-asleep, mussed up mess. That green-eyed monster who'd shown up last night, jumped back in the fray, ready to break Trent in half for seeing his man naked. Then Trent opened his mouth and he wanted to break Trent in half. Period.

"You're a faggot? Are you fucking kidding me?" Trent spat out, disgust in his voice.

"What? No, no. I'm not gay," Ford answered defensively. "He's... nothing. Never mind." It wasn't until the words fell out of his mouth, his anger getting the better of him that he realized what he'd said. The hurt in Reef's expression told Ford just how deep the words had cut. The kicker? He'd wanted to pull Trent up and knock some sense into him, explain how special Reef was to him. When Ford realized it wouldn't matter what he said, he'd stopped talking.

And now Reef thought the worst.

Whatever was growing between him and Reef was not something that needed to be explained to a homophobic bigot. There's no way he would have been on his way back to bed to cuddle Reef, to wake him up and touch him and love on him if there was nothing between them; if Reef meant nothing.

"Thanks for letting me crash, man. I'll get outta your hair," Reef pivoted and returned to the bedroom where Ford had watched him peel off his clothes the night before. Heat flashed through Ford as the memories flooded him. He stepped forward, right into Trent's outstretched arm.

"What the fuck, Trent?"

"You make me sick."

Ford got all up in Trent's face and glared at him. He only had an inch on Trent – and without shoes, the height difference was barely noticeable – but Ford had size, muscle mass. He was an intimidating fucker when he was pissed.

And he was *really* pissed.

Trent flinched when Ford narrowed his eyes and

growled at him. The prick had everything to be scared of – Ford was raging.

"Sit the fuck down and shut up, I need to see him out. Then we're gonna have a word about showing some fucking respect while you're in my house." Ford turned and began hobbling over to the bedroom as the front door slammed shut, the noise reverberating through the quiet house. Reef had just walked out. Ford didn't hesitate; he followed, going as fast as he could out the front door after him. Reef had already slammed the door of his SUV closed.

"Reef, wait!" Ford yelled, managing the step from the timber deck out front onto the pebbled drive.

He didn't stop.

Ford hung his head low and let his shoulders slump, his heart shattering as Reef drove away. He hadn't meant the words to come out sounding the way they did, certainly hadn't meant the implication. What the hell was he thinking saying bollocks like that? He hadn't been, that was the problem. He'd reacted to Trent, let his insult spark a response that he'd never normally even flinch at. Instead, he'd tried to justify their being together and insulted the man he was falling for in the process. Looking up, he watched Reef's taillights flash red as he reached the end of the street and turned left toward town. He'd fix this. He'd get Reef back. He'd explain everything. He'd make Reef see that he was the furthest thing from 'nothing' in Ford's mind and heart. But first, he needed to sort out Trent.

"I never pinned you as a fairy. Yet, you're out here weeping like a fuckin' girl over your boyfriend getting all pissy. I knew you two were goin' at it when we busted into that cabin. I'm just glad I didn't have to see you sittin' on his dick."

"Who the fuck do you think you are? Get the hell off my property and don't come back."

"Aww, the little princess has had her feelings hurt?" Ford wanted nothing more than to wipe the smirk off Trent's face with his fist, but he held onto what was important – Reef.

"Grow up, and fuck off." Ford pushed past Trent and stepped up onto the wraparound deck, opening the front door and slipping through before slamming it closed again. His morning had turned to shit so quickly. He'd imagined crawling back into bed with Reef, snuggling back down under the covers with him and wrapping his body around his. He'd wanted to kiss and lick and map each ridge and valley of muscle in his lithe body this time. Reef had loved on every inch of him and he'd wanted nothing more than to repay the favor. He closed his eyes and pictured Reef's body, the defined six pack and those cum gutters leading to the patch of trimmed dark blond hair, Reef's cock glistening with pre-cum, swollen and engorged, begging to be sucked and tasted. Would he get to touch him again? Damn straight he would. He had to.

Dialing Reef's number it rang and rang before diverting to his message service. "Reef, I'm sorry. I didn't mean it to sound like that. Please, call me back." Ford knew Reef would want some space. He wasn't going to run after the man like some stalker-freak, but he'd break out into one hell of a power-walk for a chance to catch him.

———

DIRTY LITTLE SECRET? Reef didn't fucking think so. Keep it casual, he said. Just have some fun together, he said. Sure, keep things between them but there was no hope in hell he'd be the man's dirty little secret. *Not gonna happen.* He'd been cheated on, lied to and deserted before, but never had he felt so humiliated and degraded as he did standing there naked in Ford's house being called a faggot and a 'nothing' to his face. *This* is why he'd never acted on the attraction he'd had to a man before. There was no way he was going down that road again. Nothing was worth feeling like that again.

Pulling into a parking lot in town, he walked to the lake, his footsteps crunching on the gravel at the water's edge. He'd had to go back to his hotel to get dressed. Leaving Ford's house in only last night's jeans carrying his thermal shirt had left him freezing. Having no shoes on would do that to a person too though. Reef shook his head. He'd imagined his morning taking a very different turn, one a whole lot better than it had turned out. But he was on vacation after all. At least he was going to enjoy himself. Question was, what did he want to do?

Apart from drinking until he was numb so he couldn't feel his heart being eviscerated anymore.

Dipping his fingers in, Reef marveled at how crystal clear the lake was. Tiny fish swam among the larger fist-sized rocks only a foot or two away, the icy water a hive of activity. Paddle steamers and jet boats dotted the surface and something that looked like a mechanical shark leaped in and out of the water. But despite the activity and the people, it was still peaceful. White capped mountains on the other side of the lake stood high above him. Most of the slopes looked pristine; white velvet draped over towering leviathans set against a sparkling blue sky. There was the unmistakable chill of winter in the air but it was warm too, warmer than many of the places he spent a lot of time at. He loved it here.

Reef picked up a perfect oval pebble and skimmed it across the surface of the water, watching it bounce four, five times before dropping below into the depths. That kind of felt like him at the moment, dropping, falling, drowning. Urgh, there was that fucking sap again. Reef was disgusted with himself. Why? Why did he have to go and have *feelings* for a man like Ford? Why'd he have to be attracted to men at all? And now that he'd turned it on, he couldn't reverse it. When he'd walked from the parking lot to the lake, he'd been behind a couple. She was a tall, blonde goddess with the sexiest ass he'd seen in a long time. Nothing. Nada. Then he'd looked across at the dude she was wrapped around. Tall, muscled, brown wavy hair. And waddya know? Bam. Reef's dick stood up and took notice. And that sucked even more. Not the turning it off part, but the fact that when he saw that man he pictured running his fingers through Ford's hair, pulling his body against his own, kissing him.

This time, the rock he flung into the lake was thrown, not skimmed. Anger surged through him. He hated that he was hurting, hated that he'd opened himself up and been left out in the cold. Most of all, he hated that he'd lost the chance, lost out on what he could have had with Ford. As much as he hated him right at that moment and as much as he was hurting, that damn pull he had to Ford was still there.

REEF'S MOOD still hadn't lifted by the time he made it back to the hotel. Momma Bear called and he'd ignored her. It was the first time he'd ever done that. Reef broke it off with Addilyn and the first call he'd made was to Momma Bear. She was his confidant, his friend. And yet, he was shutting her out. Now he was sitting by the roaring fire in the bar nursing his fifth scotch, lost in the dancing flames. His cell had buzzed a few times – Momma Bear checking up on him and Ford leaving a second message. Neither were easy calls to return and being three sheets to the wind didn't help. So he ignored both once again.

Last drinks were called, the lights dimmed in the bar and Reef staggered up to his room, drunk as a skunk. His cell burned a hole in his pocket. Palming it, he rolled it over and over, weighing it, tossing up what he wanted to say, whether he wanted to say anything at all. Jamming his finger down on the call button, he dialed Ford, speaking the words he needed to say as soon as Ford's tired voice came through. "You're an ass, you know that? You fucking hurt me—"

"Reef, are you drunk? Where are you?"

"Doesn't matter. I liked you. I fucking liked you."

"Reef—"

"Stop interrupting me like I'm nothing. I'm not. I'm more than that. My parents? They didn't think I was important. My ex, she thought I was worthless too. Not you. You don't get to think that. You were supposed to be different, to be more. You... you hurt me."

"Reef, I'm sorry. Please, I'm so sorry. Let me come to you."

"No, we're over."

"Reef, wait—"

"I want you. God, I want you, but you're not good for me." Reef's finger hovered over the end button when Ford's whispered voice came through again.

"I want to be more to you. Please let me." Reef's heart cracked again, his soul shattering as he ended the call and dropped his cell on the nightstand. He laid down and hugged the pillow, closing his eyes as grief like he'd never known before overwhelmed him, sadness for everything that could have been, that had started out so promising but had ended so quickly.

. . .

THE SHRILL RING of the hotel room phone woke him. Light was peeking through the drapes, but Reef couldn't look at it. His eyes burned like he'd landed a jump by face-planting into a sand dune. Cottonmouth assailed him and his head pounded. He barely managed more than a grunt when he answered it.

"Reef Reid, young man, you'd better have a good reason for ignoring my calls yesterday. You never do that."

"Don't talk so loud," he moaned.

"Are you drunk?" Momma Bear's excitement ratcheted up a notch. "Were you partying?"

"Don't remember, but I feel like shit."

"Are you with anyone? I'll hang up if you are."

Reef looked across at the undisturbed side of the bed and sighed. If Ford hadn't opened his big mouth yesterday, he would have been lying with him. But no. "I'm alone."

"Honey, what happened?"

"Been drinking. I've got a hangover."

"You don't usually get drunk. Why are you sad?" She knew him well. No one except Momma Bear would put two and two together and come to the conclusion he was upset.

"Went on a date the night before last but it didn't work out. I'm a little down about it."

Her voice softened, "Oh honey, I'm sorry. What can I do?"

"Nothing, Momma Bear. How are you and Coach doing?"

"Well, now that I've spoken to you. I've been worried about my boy. Still am."

"I'll be okay, just need to get my mind off it."

"Let me organize something special for you."

"Um, okay. If you want to."

"I promise, you'll have fun." Excitement radiated from her voice and Reef couldn't help but smile.

"Sure, why not." Reef shrugged. He didn't much care what he did. Left to his own devices, he'd probably eat, find a bar and spend the day there. Or learn to shoot. Killing a silhouette right about now sounded like a fuckin' good idea.

"Okay, check your email. I'll send you something soon. Love you, honey."

"You too, Momma Bear. Tell Coach I love him, too."

"Will do. Reef?"

"If it didn't work out, she didn't deserve you."

"Yeah, I know. I liked this one though and we had insane chemistry. Was really hoping it would."

"She's out there. You'll find her."

"Yeah. Bye, Momma Bear." Reef hung up the

phone and saw the flash of a message on his cell. Picking it up, he thumbed the screen only to see Ford's name pop up.

You were right, I'm sorry. I'll do anything to make it up to you. I know I can be good for you. Let me show you?

Reef tossed his cell to the empty spot on his bed, ignoring the cryptic message that made little sense and buried his face in the pillow again. Closing his eyes he drifted, hoping the dreams he had weren't as fucked up as the ones from the night before.

JET BOATING AND BUNGEE JUMPING – Momma Bear's idea of a good time. Reef grinned when he checked his emails a couple of hours after speaking to her. She always came through.

Showered, dressed and a hot cup of joe in his hand, Reef headed out the door to the waiting cab. They drove the short distance to the river and Reef checked-in. Suited up in a waterproof coverall, he waited with the other passengers. Around him, everyone was joking, excited about the adrenaline rush to come from skating through twelve inch deep water, bounded on either side with sheer cliffs.

They were right, it was fun. Wind whipping

around them as they hurtled around bends in the river and came within inches of the cliff face set Reef's heart racing. Flying over the water, he closed his eyes and turned his face to the sky. It was something he often did snowboarding – it was probably stupid, but Reef liked being reminded of the sheer size of the world around him; it helped put everything into context. Compared to others, the challenges he faced seemed insignificant. He had it easy. Reef had a job he loved and was pretty good at, two people who adored him like a son and a handful of friends. He was often alone, but didn't usually let it bother him. He'd always been a little disconnected from the rest of the world; he could cope with that too. He and Ford, well, maybe it just wasn't meant to be. Still hurt though.

Bungee jumping was even better than he expected. The air he got snowboarding always gave him a rush, but this was something else. Jumping off the bridge was crazy fun. He had a goofy smile on his face the whole way down. The elastic rope tied around his ankles stretched taut and bounced him back up, only to give him a few more seconds of free fall. Each time, the free fall lessened until he was dangling upside down waiting to be taken down.

"Fuckin' awesome, man. Thanks." He laughed, shaking the attendant's hand. "What a rush."

"Yeah, most people enjoy it. You didn't hesitate when you jumped. Bit of an adrenaline junkie?"

"Yeah, you could say that." He nodded.

"You can go skydiving too, you know? And heli-skiing if you're a good enough skier."

"Yeah, think I'll try them out." Reef grinned at him again and waved as the attendant turned his attention to the next person coming off after her jump.

HE FOUND himself eating dinner at a bar and downing a few beers. The night progressed and Reef watched from the sidelines. Music pumped through the speakers – Justin Bieber's latest, apparently – had bodies writhing, but he wasn't feelin' it. He wasn't feeling much of anything. Drunk again, the flashing lights and light-headedness made the room spin and Reef nauseous. Ignoring it, Reef ordered another round for himself and the three girls that had joined him. They were out for some fun. And he wanted to forget, to dull the pain in his chest that had started when a remix of a Sam Smith heartbreak song started playing.

Standing at the bar, Reef found himself holding his cell again, this time spinning it on the dark timber surface. The urge to speak to Ford, to hear his voice again pulsed through Reef. Ford had left two more messages that day, texting him again a few more times. Reef had a few things he needed to say. Stepping into the men's room, Reef dialed him.

"You've wormed your way into my head and I can't fucking get it up without thinking of you—"

"You drunk again, Reef?"

"Yeah, I'm wasted." Reef sighed. "I miss you, Ford."

"I miss you, too. Where are you?"

"A bar. Not sure which one."

"Can I meet you somewhere?"

"No. Don't want... to want you." He sighed. That was the crux of it. He didn't want to want Ford, but the man was under his skin. He'd known him for less than a week but in that time, they'd connected. And there was no doubt that Reef wanted him in his bed. Just talking to him gave him a hard-on.

"I know. I'm sorry, Reef. I know it sounds lame, but I didn't mean things how they sounded. You're important to me."

"Yeah, well it's too late." Reef could hear the slur in his voice but he didn't care. He was pouting, pouring on the self-pity.

"Where are you staying, Reef?" He blurted out the hotel before he could help himself. "Go there. Get some sleep. When you want to talk and you aren't drunk, call me. I'll give you space, but only so much, Reef. I want you and I'm not giving up."

"I wanna forget you, Ford."

"Too bad. I'm not letting you go. There's something about you. Me and you—"

"Yeah, I think I already know that. That's what scares me." He hung up uncertain of everything now, but knowing he didn't want to be in the club anymore. Taking the drinks back to the table, he said his good-byes and left, taking a deep breath of the crisp night air. Reef walked back to the lake and sat on a large boulder at the water's edge. He watched the dark swirls from the feeding fish as the chill cleared his drunken haze. What had he done? He'd just drunk dialed Ford.

Oh, fuck.

Shaking his head, Reef closed his eyes and rested his forehead in the heel of his hands. He was painfully honest when drunk. Like zero filter. He was a menace to himself. Palming his cell again, he checked the call registry. Two days, two calls. Ford, both times. What did Reef say the first time? Groaning, he picked himself up and began the short walk back to his hotel. He dared not check any of his social media profiles. It was embarrassing the truth of some of the utter bullshit he posted about when he was wasted.

And now he was painfully sober. What a fuckin' disaster.

IT HAD BEEN five days since he'd spoken with Ford and Reef couldn't work up the courage to call him. Embarrassment reigned supreme. He'd spent the week doing more of the touristy things – a *Lord of the Rings* tour, eating a burger from the famed burger joint that had a twenty minute wait just to put in an order—and it was worth every second of that wait—going fishing on the lake. But those were nothing more than time-fillers. He couldn't get into anything the way he should have. His mind was preoccupied with Ford. Sitting in the modern wingback chair by the fire in the lobby bar, Reef nursed a coffee. He let out a sigh. He knew what he wanted to do, but did he really have the courage to open himself up?

"That sounds ominous," a woman's voice sounded from beside him. Her accent had a beautiful drawl to it, which was purely from the US southern states. Recognition dawned. He knew that voice: the lady with the long auburn hair, endless curves and purple boots from the airport.

"You have no idea." Reef smiled while standing

and offering her the chair opposite him. "Sorry, I'm hopeless with names. What was yours again?"

"Cassie Lane. We saw you sitting here. Thought we'd come say hi. Jos will be here in a minute; he's getting drinks. You're Reef, right?"

"Yeah. Enjoying your trip?"

"We are, I'm learning to ski. So far I haven't broken anything, so I'm happy." She laughed. Sobering, she added, "Are you? Enjoying your trip? Happy? You look awfully down for someone who's on vacation."

"Eh." He shrugged non-committedly. He didn't want to talk about his problems.

"That's okay, just thought I'd offer."

"It's been a rough couple of weeks. You know how it goes: you meet someone, go out on a date, have it not work out, drunk dial them, the whole nine yards. It wasn't pretty."

"Ouch."

"Tell me about it."

"How'd she take it?"

Reef sighed again. "He. Not she. The fucked up thing is that I'm straight. Or at least I thought I was until I met Ford. He's... Damn, I have no idea how to explain it."

"An immediate connection, like you knew you had to be together."

"I... yeah. How did you know?"

"My boyfriend and I. It was crazy. Within thirty seconds of knowing him, I knew. We fell into bed together, but then lost contact. Six months later I ran into him out of the blue." As she spoke, the same man who he'd seen her with at the airport, placed a mug on the table and handed Cassie the other.

"Here you go, Angel." Turning to Reef, he stuck out his hand waiting for Reef to shake it. "I'm Jos Farris. Mind if we join you?"

"Not at all," Reef replied, rising again to grip Jos' hand. "I'm Reef Reid." Speaking to both of them, Reef added, "Your story's pretty amazing."

"The six months we were apart were hell. I'd fallen in love with Cass, but I had no way of contacting her. I tried everything, but she thought I didn't want to see her again. "

"It all worked out in the end, though."

"Yeah, and we couldn't be happier." Cassie smiled at Jos, leaning into him as he hugged her close and kissed her temple. Seeing them together, seeing the love that flowed between the two of them, made Reef even more aware of how much he wanted Ford.

"Ford said something that hurt, really hurt. I believed him when he told me that he didn't mean it like it sounded. Afterwards, he said he was serious about me. When we were together... I believed his body, his reactions. But, I don't know. Sorry, this is TMI."

Cassie waved her hand like she was dismissing Reef's concerns and smiled. "I work with a group of women who believe in sharing every detail of their sex lives. This isn't too much. My advice? Contact him, talk to him. If the two of you feel strongly enough about each other, don't walk away. Fight for each other. Fight for your own happiness."

"For what it's worth, I agree," Jos added, nodding encouragingly at Reef.

"Thank you," Reef replied softly. He toasted them with his coffee mug and took another drink of the cooling liquid. Fight for Ford. Fight for himself. Fight for them. It sounded easy, but could Reef do it? He had to, he had no choice. Reef had fallen hard, so much so, that he hadn't stopped thinking of Ford since the moment they'd met. It was time to go and take back what he wanted.

CHAPTER EIGHT

Five days. Five fuckin' days, and he hadn't heard from him. Reef hadn't returned any of his calls or messages. Well, apart from the two drunk as a skunk, slurred conversations. And the radio silence was starting to piss Ford off. It was time he stepped things up and got his man back. Hell yeah, *his man*. His plan would work. It had to. He needed Reef to understand he wasn't going away. Ford had given him all the space he was gonna get.

Pulling his truck up to the hotel Reef was staying at, he limped over to reception. "Hi, ah, I'm a friend of one of your guests. I'm not sure what room he's in, but I was hoping you could call up and let him know he has a guest. Reef Reid."

"Sir, he's just arrived in the lobby bar. His other guest arrived a little while ago."

"Oh, okay. Thanks." Ford's brow creased. Was he too late? Dammit, he shouldn't have given Reef that much space. Regretting every move he'd made since he left his bed that fateful morning, he went over to the bar. Ford liked this hotel, he'd used it as inspiration for his own house. Stone walls lined one side of the room while the other was floor-to-ceiling windows overlooking Lake Wakatipu and the Remarkables Ranges. The high roof was all exposed dark timber beams and wrought iron light fittings that looked like wagon-wheels with candles mounted on them. Timber skis and poles, sleds and Maori weapons and tools lined the walls together with pictures of the historical fishing trawlers that hauled their catches onto the docks.

In a cozy spot in the corner tucked in close to the stone fireplace sat Reef one ankle crossed over his other knee, fingers wrapped around a tumbler filled with a finger of amber liquid and ice. He looked disinterested as a woman talked animatedly. Ford could tell she was beautiful, even with her back to him. Long platinum blonde hair cascaded down her back, hanging lightly over a ridiculously thick white coat with a fur collar. It was like she had a serious objection to the cold. "Oh, fuck no. He's not back with her."

As Ford stepped toward them, Reef looked up meeting his gaze. His face lit up briefly that perfect kissable mouth breaking into a grin and showing his sexy-as-sin dimples, his rich brown eyes sparkling. It only lasted a second before he schooled his features, but in that moment Ford knew he still had a chance.

"Hey," he murmured softly to Reef as he pulled up a chair without asking.

"Excuse me, do you mind? We're having a private conversation."

Turning to the blonde, he looked her up and down. She was unmistakably Addilyn, Reef's ex. He'd recognize that pout and – even in her early twenties – her perfectly botoxed face. Ford raised an eyebrow at her and replied, "Oh I'm sorry, I didn't realize you were here. I was meeting Reef." Leaning into his man, he smiled and asked, "I know I'm not your favorite person at the moment, but I'd like to make it up to you. Can I?"

Reef looked at him long and hard. He supposed it was to see whether there was any hesitation, any denial in what Ford wanted. There wasn't. There was no denying it anymore. He wanted so much more than casual when it came to Reef.

"A proper date, candlelit dinner, wine if you want, watching the sunset together. The works," he added.

"Yeah?" Reef asked with a smile, his eyes darting to Addilyn before he turned his attention back to Ford. Ford's heart soared, he hadn't been shot down in flames yet.

"Yeah, sweet cheeks. Whatever you want."

"Okay." Reef nodded and smiled again, Ford's world lighting up at the warmth in those big browns that locked on his. Without thinking, Ford reached out and grasped his hand, linking their fingers together.

"What the fuck?" Addilyn asked, the shock and indignity in her voice evident. "You can't just ditch me for him. I flew across the world to see you."

"Addilyn, we've spoken about this. We're not getting back together, now or ever. I don't trust you. I don't even like you anymore, never mind being attracted to you."

"You can't just walk away from what we had."

"You walked away the moment you hopped into bed with your photographers."

"We were *so* good together."

"No, we really weren't. Don't you get it? You had sex with what three, four different men while we were dating? That's not being *so good together*."

"I was alone, lonely. You pushed me to do it."

Reef snorted and shook his head. "In the thirty minutes we've been sitting here, you haven't told me once how you feel about me, you haven't even given me one good reason why I should be sitting here. All you've spoken about is your career, what label you're modeling for next week, next month. I don't know why you want me back and I don't care." Reef looked at Ford and smiled, before turning back to her, pinning her with eyes that were deadly serious. "It ain't happening. We're done."

"So what? You're suddenly gay?"

Reef squeezed Ford's hand and the warm fuzzies that shot through his body at the touch made the ache in his chest match the one in his cock. "I'm bi."

"Since when?"

"Does it matter? We're over, we're not getting back together. The rest of it is none of your business."

"So what am I supposed to do now?"

"We're in a hotel. Go see if they have a room."

"Reef." Addilyn pleaded.

"No. You came here to try and talk me back into a relationship that I don't want. You took the risk flying out on a whim when you found out where I was staying. You made your bed." Reef turned from Addilyn and Ford knew instantly that he was through with his ex. All Reef's attention was now focused on him. The intensity of their connection blew him away.

"You wanna head out now, or you want a drink

first?" Ford asked Reef, squeezing his hand as they stood.

"I need to get ready for my date. Can I meet you back here in fifteen?"

"Sure. You aren't disappearing are you, leaving from a back exit?"

Reef shook his head and grasped the lapels of Ford's suit jacket, drawing Ford to him. His automatic reaction was to wrap his arms around Reef, hold him close. To touch his man. "I was gonna call you but got interrupted. Cassie made me realize that I was done trying to forget you."

"You can fill me in on who Cassie is later."

"Met her at the airport. She and her boyfriend, Jos, are staying here. I was here having a coffee and ran into her. We got talking. Then she showed up." Reef nodded toward Addilyn who was still there.

"I really want to kiss you right now," Ford murmured, zeroing in on Reef's full lips.

"What are you waiting for?" Reef smiled softly, straightening out Ford's lapel once more.

Leaning in, Ford brushed his lips against Reef's, the touch whisper soft, before resting their foreheads together.

"I missed you."

"Me too. More than you know. Go, get changed. I wanna take you out."

Reef winced. "I left my suit jacket at your house. Can we swing by there?"

"It's in the car with the rest of the clothes you left behind. I'll go get it."

"Hey, you don't have your crutches." Reef only just noticed.

"I stopped using them a couple of days ago."

"Good, glad you're getting better. I, ah... should go get dressed."

"Go." Ford smiled, letting Reef go. Running his hands down Ford's chest, Reef stepped away quickly walking out of the bar.

"Unfuckingbelievable." Addilyn spoke from next to him.

"What? That you aren't the center of attention?" Ford turned to regard her. He'd forgotten she was even there, Reef consuming his consciousness.

"He's in love with you. He never once looked at me like that. With that... adoration."

"I don't deserve him. But I'll work as hard as I can to get there."

"Don't fail him. He's a good man." Addilyn regarded him closely again and shook her head before sashaying away. The relief that coursed through Ford almost buckled his knees. The crisis that was Reef's ex was averted. If the rest of the night with Reef went as well, he'd be a happy man.

"HEY," Reef said shyly as he stepped up next to Ford. Dressed in black slacks and a white button down shirt, he looked damn good. Edible.

"You look fuckin' hot. Ready?"

"Yeah. Where are we going?"

"You been up the gondola, yet?"

"No, it kinda feels like a couple-thing to do."

"Good, that's where we're going. I'm wining and dining you and we're watching the sunset together."

"You gonna expect me to put out after all that? I'm not easy you know." Reef grinned at him, his perfect white teeth and those sexy as fuck dimples flashing.

"We go at your pace."

"Well, I'm hungry so let's eat." Reef grabbed Ford's hand and began walking before his steps faltered. "Um, where am I going?"

"Out the front door. My truck's parked outside."

THEY DROVE the few minutes to their destination in comfortable silence. Hand in hand they walked to the gondolas and hopped on, facing the view as the cable car rose higher up the side of the mountain. The late afternoon sun shone down on the picturesque village, glinting off the white caps in the distance. Clouds rolling in over the mountains signaled another snow dump was coming. "Hey, selfie time. I want pics to remember my vacation." Reef held out his cell and clicked a shot of them; heads together, grinning like love-struck teenagers. Ford grabbed it out of his hands and kissed Reef's face, taking another photo.

"Aww, you romantic." Reef teased. Ford cupped his cheek and licked the length of his face, clicking off another few shots. Reef laughed loudly and pressed their lips together, as Ford depressed the shutter again. Deepening their kiss, their tongues stroking, lips melding together, Ford's arms wrapping around Reef's lithe body. Cell forgotten, Ford dropped it on the seat between them as he chased Reef's tongue once more. Reef combed his fingers through his hair and tugged on the curls. Their moans punctuated the air. Hot, heavy breaths washed against his cheek as Ford broke the kiss and nipped his way along Reef's jawline.

"Maybe dinner was a bad idea," Reef moaned.

"No. Need to show you how much you mean."

"You can do that naked."

"It's not about me wanting you. You know that.

Want the world to see it too." Ford pressed their lips together again as the gondola slowed, coasting into the mountaintop station. "Come on, lemmie show you one of the best views in town." Grasping Reef's hand again, they climbed out of the cable car, grateful for the suit jacket that hid the evidence of his arousal. The afternoon air that met them was cool, a crisp breeze blowing over the snow covered peaks.

Reef leaned against the timber railing, looking out over the vista below them. "I love this place. It's so easy to wanna stay."

"Would you come back? After your comp season."

"Are you asking?"

"Maybe." Ford smiled at him. Nerves exploded through his body. Was he really asking that? Was he asking Reef to change something so dramatic about his life so they could be together?

"Then yes. I've always gone to South America to extend my season but I could train here. What about you? You thinking of going back to Italy when you finish up here?"

"Yeah, unless you can suggest somewhere else."

"I do preseason training in Canada but Italy's good. Easy to get to." Reef smiled and leaned into Ford's shoulder, pressing their bodies closer together. Ford didn't hesitate, kissing him below his ear and wrapping his arms around Reef again, Reef's back to his front. The knowledge that they'd keep seeing each other after Reef's vacation ended changed things for the better. There was no longer any doubt about where this was heading, and casual wasn't it.

"TOBOGGANS?" Reef asked excitedly.

"Yeah, they're fun. Wanna share one?"

"Hell yeah. Let's go." Chuckling, Ford tugged on Reef's hand drawing him to the toboggan chairlift.

Reaching the top, they sat down together, Reef in front directing the steering and pedals, Ford holding onto him. They flew down the track, bumping the sides and taking corners faster than they should have, laughing and smack talking the other riders. Wind ruffled Ford's hair as he held onto the man he was falling hard and fast for. No, that wasn't right. Ford had already fallen, of that there was no doubt.

Dinner was in the restaurant at the top of the peak with the perfect panoramic view below. He hadn't thought to book a table, but Ford was lucky. It was a Tuesday, so the restaurant was quieter than the weekend. They scored a table right by the full-height windows, watching the sun sink behind the ranges, and the lights below them twinkle to life. As the light faded from the sky and twilight turned into night, they moved onto dessert, a waiter discreetly placing the chocolate sampler plate between them.

"Oh hell yeah," Ford moaned. "I could come on the spot."

"I'm so fuckin' hard right now. Watching the way you eat that chocolate, rolling your tongue around it as you taste it. So fuckin' erotic."

"You should have some too. Taste this." Ford picked up a miniature chocolate cup and brought it up to Reef's lips. Biting down on the dessert, Reef's eyes closed and a low moan sounded in his throat. *Fucking hell*. Sexiest. Sound. *Ever*. Ford's cock stood to attention and his body ached to pull Reef into his arms, get naked and taste every inch of him.

"Coffee cups. These ones are peppermint, I think." Ford bit down on the after dinner mint Reef held up to his lips.

"Mmhmm," Ford rumbled low in his throat as Reef's fingers brushed across his lips. Unable to resist the treat, he swiped his tongue across the digits and watched as Reef's pupils dilated. Heat flared in those warm brown orbs.

They continued like that, feeding each other tit-for-tat until the sampler tray was empty. Ford was so worked up he could barely see straight. Desperate for release he almost cried when Reef suggested they have a coffee before they go. His pouting disappeared at Reef's cheeky grin. He stood and held his hand out to Ford.

"It was a joke. Take me to your place. I feel like putting out."

Ford tossed a few bills down on the table with the check as Reef reached for his wallet. "No, my treat," he murmured before pulling Reef into a fast, hard kiss.

They barely made the ride down the cable car with clothes intact. Tumbling onto the seat, Reef straddled him as his mouth came down and possessed Ford's in a kiss that left them both breathless. Hands under Reef's shirt, Ford kneaded the length of his muscular back down to his firm ass. Pulling him against his aching cock, Reef ground down upon him. Moans filled the air as they rocked together, their tongues tangling. Reef's hands fisting his hair had him gasping for breath. As the car slowed and it jolted into the station, they forced a sliver a space between them.

"I need to get you home and naked in my bed a-sap," Ford growled.

"Amen to that."

CRASHING THROUGH THE FRONT DOOR, Reef's jacket fell to the floor only a moment before he kicked off his shoes and Ford tore open his shirt, buttons bouncing off the walls. Ford's mouth was magic on his. Hot, desperate, wild. Unrestrained passion.

The leather belt was yanked from its loops and tossed aside, while the button was quickly loosened and the zipper pulled down. Ford's big hand gripped Reef's aching cock, stroking him, ripping a moan from Reef.

"Oh, god. You feel so good, Ford."

"I need to taste you, Reef." The rest of their clothes were stripped from their bodies as they tumbled into the bedroom, landing on the king sized bed. Fully naked and looming over him, Ford was magnificent. Every inch of his pale skin glowed in the moonlight being cast through the window. He was an Adonis, perfectly sculpted muscles bunching and flexing as he held himself on his forearms above Reef. His blue eyes were dark and those lips called to him.

"You are one sexy motherfucker, you know that, Ford?"

"Never thought I'd say it out loud about a man, but bloody hell, Reef, I can't get enough of you. Sexy doesn't even come close."

As Ford lowered his mouth, Reef captured those perfect lips. Ford didn't just kiss him, he possessed him. Tangling his fingers in those curls Reef couldn't get enough of, he tugged Ford closer. Lips melding, tongues caressing, flirting together, Reef kissed his man with everything he had. Their naked bodies pressed tight, grinding and loving on one another. Reef ran his foot up Ford's leg, the crisp hairs the complete opposite of what he was used to. Hard muscles in place of curves teased him as Reef used his hands to wander over and explore Ford's smooth, wide back. Running his fingers down Ford's spine, Reef worked the hot spots at the joins of Ford's muscles until he was jerking against him.

"Fuck, you've got to stop. I'm gonna come, and I wanna taste you."

"God, that accent, Ford. It gets stronger when you're turned on and fuck me dead if it doesn't make me hotter for you," Reef moaned as Ford nipped his way along his jaw to that sensitive spot below his ear. He bit down on it and a rush of breath left Reef. "Ford, oh god." He thrust his hips, desperate for more friction against his pulsing shaft.

Ford tasted every inch of him, licking and biting, laying open mouthed kisses on the entire length of his body which was absolutely vibrating with need. Never

ever had Reef been loved on like that. No one had mapped every muscle, every dip and curve of his body in the way Ford did. They'd talked about a future together, they'd fooled around before but this was on another level. Ford showed him with every touch, with every caress that he was cherished.

Reef cried out as Ford bit down on his hip bone, his neck arching back as he raced toward the edge of orgasm. A bead of pre-cum leaked from his cockhead, dripping down to smear a path along his taut belly. Ford's moan had Reef's eyes focusing, watching as he licked the clear liquid from his skin. Reef shuddered as a warm breath ghosted over his dick before Ford and that magical tongue of his licked another path from root to tip. Following the vein on the underside of his cock, Ford ran his lips over Reef's shaft, without breaking their gaze. He watched as Ford knelt between his open legs, pushing them further apart to fit his shoulders between Reef's knees.

"You need to tell me what you like. I've never done this before," Ford whispered, a hint of uncertainty in his voice.

"Play with my balls, fist my cock if you don't wanna suck it, but keep your face close. I wanna feel your breath on me, your stubble on my legs."

"Guide me?"

Gripping his underarms, Reef hauled Ford up. Meeting him half way in a crunch, he kissed Ford with all he had, sliding their tongues together as their lips joined.

"I just want you, that's enough. But I'll fuckin' love on you so hard if you suck my cock."

Ford chuckled, his nervousness seeming to break just as Reef had hoped. He slid back down Reef's body and licked around the head of his shaft. Moaning quietly, Ford's eyes fluttered closed as his lips opened and he took Reef in, inch by inch. His tongue worked Reef like a champion, lapping and gettin' frisky with the sensitive spot just below his corona. Reef couldn't stop the noises coming from him. Moaning, he fisted Ford's hair, fighting against the instinct to thrust into the warm wet cavern of his mouth.

"Holy fuck, Ford. Don't stop."

Ford reached out tentatively and touched his nuts, running his thumb down the seam of Reef's sac. Kneading and rolling them, Reef stiffened. His cock thickened further, pre-cum leaking from his slit as he panted, riding the knife-edge of a killer orgasm. When Ford's other hand joined in, fisting the base of Reef's cock, he had no hope.

"Gonna come," he moaned.

Ford pulled off at the last second and breathed

deep, continuing his slow stroking of Reef's cock as Reef cried out in frustration. "Don't want you to come, yet," Ford murmured as he lay open mouthed kisses along Reef's inner thighs, letting Reef recompose himself. He grunted in response to Ford's comment, unable to put into words how fuckin' good Ford's stubble felt against his sensitive skin. Delving back in, Ford licked him like a lollipop before sucking him down deeper than he had before. He applied the perfect amount of suction, just the right amount of twist each time he lifted his head. Need curled in Reef's gut and exploded as Ford's fingers brushed his ass. Choking out a cry, Reef couldn't stop the instinctive thrust of his hips.

"Ford, please." Reef begged, not really knowing what he needed. Desperation swamped him.

"What do you want, Reef?"

"I... I don't know. I just—" Reef's words halted as Ford's fingers brushed his ass again.

"You want me to play with your ass?"

"Yesss," he hissed as Ford traced the line of his crack with a blunt fingertip. "Nghunhn," Reef grunted as Ford wiggled his fingers, touching them against his hole.

"Reef?" Ford paused waiting until his glazed eyes focused on him. "You want this? Are you ready for it?"

"God, yes. Do it, Ford. I... I need you in me." Reef let the words tumble out of him, exhaling on a rush. Ford performed some serious acrobatics to get the lube and a condom from the top drawer of his bedside table without shifting off Reef. He could have laughed at Ford's lightning fast reaction. Instead, Reef licked the length of Ford's obliques with a smile, biting down on his hip in the same way Ford had done to him.

"Ford, kiss me," Reef murmured, when Ford hovered above him again. Gripping the back of his neck, he pulled him closer. Reef's eyes fluttered closed when Ford licked his bottom lip, sucking the plump flesh in. Wet fingers circled his opening and Reef gasped, Ford taking the opportunity to lick into Reef's mouth, deepening their kiss.

Pulling back, Ford murmured against Reef's throat, "If this hurts, tell me. It didn't look like it was supposed to."

"Huh?" Reef asked, being pulled from a lust-filled haze.

"Porn. I watched a fuck-load of porn this week."

"Nghunhn," Reef grunted again as the image of Ford jacking off to porn flashed before his eyes.

"You like that, don't you? Knowing that you've turned me inside out, knowing that I got off watching men come, picturing you instead."

Ford rimmed him again before pushing a blunt fingertip into his ass. Reef tensed, hissing as pain shot through him.

"Breathe, sweet. Bear down a little on my finger. Let me in." He did, sucking in a breath and relaxing his muscles. Ford popped his finger past the resistance and thrust gently in and out. The sensation was completely new to him, full and taboo, but intimate on a level he'd never experienced. It was even better than his fantasies.

"So fuckin' strange."

"Good strange or bad?"

"Good. Go deeper." He panted before Ford joined their mouths together and finger-fucked him deeper, harder, just like he'd asked. Reef writhed in pleasure, stiffening when something deep within him was touched, lighting him up like fireworks. Ford pulled back, adding a second then a third finger to the mix, increasing the fullness within Reef.

"Ford," he moaned again. "Want you in me." Ford pulled back and they stared at each other. Reef was awed. The man before him was gorgeous, sexy mussed up hair, eyes the deepest blue, lips swollen from their kisses, every defined muscle on his body tensed as he held himself above Reef. The raw emotion in his expression had Reef's heart filling. He wasn't prepared to label it, but whatever it was, he knew they were both in the same place.

"I know, Ford. Me too," Reef whispered as he cupped Ford's cheek before lifting his head up off the bed to eliminate the distance between himself and Ford, kissing him softly.

"Yeah, me too." Ford rolled the condom on and Reef held out his hand, palm up. Sticky liquid dribbled onto his palm and he gripped Ford's shaft, Reef lubing him up. He watched as Ford drizzled some onto his own fingers before wrapping his hand around Reef's aching cock and doing the same.

"Make me yours. Become mine."

Looking down at their bodies, Reef watched as Ford, propped up on one elbow, lined himself up at Reef's entrance. Reef lifted his ass up off the bed as Ford pushed in an inch, joining them together. It burned, but the pressure quickly morphed into neediness. "More, Ford. Please," he begged. Ford thrust gently, gliding in an inch or two before retreating and pushing forward again. Each time he moved, he hit Reef's prostate.

"Holy fuck, Ford. Harder."

Ford bottomed out, pressing his hips tight against Reef's ass. Reef was overwhelmed by Ford's touch – his cock, his hands trailing up his leg to Reef's hip, pausing to give him a gentle squeeze before continuing up to Reef's nipple and tweaking it. Their mouths crashed together while their tongues danced. Reef was blissed out of his mind. That fullness should have felt weird. The thought of another man's cock being buried inside him should have freaked him out, but sex had never felt so good. Ford's touch was firm, but gentle at the same time. His big body covered him, embracing him in a way that made Reef never want to let go. Wrapping his arms and legs around Ford, Reef did exactly that – he held on tight. Their mouths smashed together, their tongues dueling in a fierce contest for dominance as Ford began moving. What started out as long slow strokes, soon became frantic thrusts, Reef instinctively knowing that they were both nearing the edge. The burn in Reef's ass increased, the sparks of lightning at the base of his spine radiating outwards, as every one of Ford's thrusts unerringly hit that magic spot. Reef pressed the point on Ford's back that he knew sent him wild, bringing their bodies closer together. His cock surged between them, rubbing against Ford's ripped abs with each of his thrusts. It was as if a tight fist grasped Reef. His shaft pulsed as his ass was hammered. Reef's senses went into over-load, every one heightened. Even the hairs on Ford's body rubbing against his skin sent explosions of sensation through him. Heavy breaths on his neck and his own moans, filled the air. Ford bit down on his throat as Reef speared his fingers through the curls at the nape of Ford's neck. That rough touch, the bite of pain and zing of fire that streaked through Reef as Ford thrust his hips forward again, hitting his prostate dead-on, sent him over the edge. Reef shouted as hot ribbons of cum pumped from his cock. His ass clamped down and jet after jet shot out of him, emptying his release between them. Ford stiffened above him and roared as he filled the condom with his orgasm. As Ford slumped down on top of him, Reef ran his fingertips down his back to cup his ass. Breathlessly, he turned his face toward Ford and kissed him, their tongues doing a lazy dance as they melded their mouths together.

"Need to toss out the condom," Ford murmured against his lips.

"Not yet," Reef whispered against his skin, breathing Ford's unique scent in deep. He licked at a bead of sweat which had formed at Ford's temple and was running down his cheek. Laying open mouthed kisses along his stubbly jaw, Reef hummed as Ford turned his face and kissed him back, his softened cock slipping out of Reef's depths. Rolling them to the side, Ford pulled off the used condom, tossing it to the floor. Wrapped around each other, they held each other tight, making out and murmuring softly as they came down from their high.

———

FORD HAD NEVER HAD that level of intimacy before, never had sex held so much meaning. Usually it was a way to get off, a needed release. He'd never been much of a cuddler afterwards, but with Reef it was natural. He didn't want to let his man go, but he needed to care for him. Reef had to be sore and the need sparked within Ford to make him as comfortable as possible. He pulled back but Reef held him tighter. Ford relaxed against him understanding that, for the moment, contact was what Reef needed. And if Reef didn't mind the mess, Ford sure as hell wasn't going to pull away. As Neanderthal as it sounded, he'd marked Reef as his, in the same way that Reef's cum now marked him. That possessive flare – that need to give himself over and get Reef in return – was sated knowing the man in his arms wasn't going anywhere. Giving into exhaustion, Ford let his eyelids droop and he nuzzled into Reef's shoulder, holding him tight.

CHAPTER NINE

FORD STARTLED at Reef's hiss of pain. "You okay, sweet cheeks?" he murmured, half asleep.

"Yeah," he groaned. "Little sore." That had Ford opening his eyes, sleep the farthest thing from his mind.

"Come on, let me get you in the Jacuzzi. The heat will help."

Ford snatched up a condom and the bottle of lube before they padded naked to the deck at the back of the house, hand in hand, and slipped into the hot water. Relaxing back, Ford pulled Reef into his arms, resting his chin on his lover's shoulder.

"It's gorgeous out here. Damn, even at night there's a hell of a view." Reef was right. The whitecaps on the mountains reflected the moonlight, lighting up the sky on one side of the small yard. To the other, the land sloped away from them opening up a view of a carpet of twinkling lights from Queenstown. It was Ford's piece of paradise. He'd been saving to buy the farm ever since his first season in Queenstown. When the developers moved in and the value of the land skyrocketed, he thought he'd lost his chance until he saw they were building a land estate. He'd signed up as soon as the plots went on the market, designing and building his cottage soon after. This land, his very own little slice of the world, was what kept him returning to the same ski resort year after year. Nothing compared to going home after months away in Italy each year. Having Reef there completed it. Ford had never pictured settling down and sharing this space with anyone, but now he couldn't imagine anything else.

"You want to give up that hotel room and stay with me until you leave?" Ford knew he was impulsive, but when the words slipped out of his mouth even he thought his request was a little crazy. And yet, Ford wasn't freaking out. He smiled, knowing that being with Reef was exactly what he wanted, no matter how soon, no matter how nuts it seemed.

"You're kidding, right?" Reef turned in his arms, running his fingertips over Ford's collarbone.

"Only if you don't want to stay." Ford shrugged,

trying to downplay the importance of the question. Nerves buzzed through him in anticipation of Reef's answer. He had no idea until that moment how much he wanted Reef to say yes.

"Don't do that, Ford. Don't make light of your feelings." Reef kissed Ford's throat, his cheeks, his nose, his lips. "I'd really like that."

"You would?"

"Yeah, I really wanna stay with you." Reef leaned forward and kissed him again, his tongue seeking entry as Ford wrapped his legs around Reef's waist. Holding him tight with one arm, Reef made love to his mouth. Sliding his hand between them, he worshipped Ford's body with the other, enveloping both their shafts in his hand, pumping them lazily as they hardened again. Ford shivered as Reef slipped his other hand down to his ass, kneading the muscle and running his finger along his crack. Reef massaged his rosebud, pressing and loosening the muscle, without delving in, all the while stroking them together. Reef teased him as Ford thrust into the tight grip.

"Do it, sweet," Ford moaned.

"Wanna try something else. Roll over, ass up outta the water."

Ford moved around bending over and presenting his

ass to Reef, watching his every move over his shoulder. When the man licked his lips, Ford's cock pulsed in anticipation. Reef traced his tongue along Ford's inner thigh and along his sac. The movement nearly had Ford jumping out of his skin. That tongue was magic. Whether it was the way he spoke—all deep with a smooth, sexy American accent—or the way he kissed, gettin' all playful with Ford's tongue, or the way he was licking his perineum. It was taboo, something Ford shouldn't want, but which only seemed to turn him on more. Pressing his ass back, he whimpered when Reef pulled away chuckling.

Warm breaths ghosted against his wet skin. "You weren't the only one watching porn, Ford. Getting you under me is a fuckin' wet dream."

Ford's cry echoed throughout the quiet landscape as Reef brought his mouth down to his pucker, laying open-mouthed kisses and licks against him. Soft suction had him bucking into Reef's firm hold. Stiffening his tongue, Reef rimmed his outer muscles before penetrating Ford the smallest amount which nearly sent him flying.

"Holy fuck," Ford panted, clamping his fist around his cock to stop from blowing like a bottle rocket. Reef hummed against his skin, turning Ford on even more. Long slow strokes, quick laps, circles lashed around his rim had Ford moving his fist, jacking off to the hottest thing he'd ever experienced.

"Need more, Reef. Gimme your fingers." The lube Ford tossed to the side when they'd gone outside was snatched up and Ford closed his eyes, listening to the sound of Reef squeezing the clear liquid onto his fingers. Coolness pressed against him, and that tongue was back, licking at his perineum. Ford exhaled, focusing on relaxing his sphincter as Reef pushed harder, moving past his resistance and sliding in further. He pushed back, fucking himself on Reef's digit as Reef curled his finger, the pad brushing against his prostate. Ford's moans and jerky movements caused Reef to press harder against the spongy bundle of nerves, shooting lightning bolts through him. Ecstasy built quickly until Ford's hips were stuttering, fighting to reach the peak that only a moment ago wasn't yet within reach. A second finger was added, intensifying the sensations spinning through Ford. Reef licked him where his fingers plunged in, pushing him until he was on the knife's edge of erupting.

"Fuck, tell me you're ready." Reef breathed against his skin, only pausing in his ministrations to utter the words.

"Yes, get in me now. I need you, Reef." Ford writhed, desperate to fall into that abyss of ecstasy, but wanting to prolong the climb for as long as possible. The tearing of a foil wrapper sounded from behind him and Reef's body disappeared momentarily. A large hand pressed down on Ford's lower back holding him in place as Reef lined his cock up with Ford's opening. Exhale. Relax. Burn. Fuuuck. Ford tensed at the shot of fire that ran through him when his ass was stretched wider than he'd ever imagined it could be.

Instantly, the burn was gone and the warmth of Reef's chest blanketed his back. Strong arms wrapped around him and a rough hand jacked him off as soft kisses were pressed at the nape of his neck.

"S'okay, hon. Deep breath in, slow out. Do it with me," Reef murmured. Ford copied him, letting Reef take the reins and guide him through the experience. Fingers buried in him again, stretching him once more. Each muscle in his back unknotted slowly and Reef pulled his fingers free, replacing them once again with the head of his thick shaft. "Breathe again, Ford." Kisses peppered his shoulders and neck and Reef pushed forward, breaching him. The burn wasn't bad this time. As Reef worked inside him, he hit his g-spot like he'd found moments ago with his fingers. The difference in intensity between Reef's digits and his dick had Ford choking out a cry. Reef pushed forward again, bottoming out inside his ass before pulling back slightly.

"Hold still. Gimme a minute, or I'm gonna blow," Ford begged, one hand on Reef's muscular ass holding him tight.

A second later Ford was pushing back, impaling himself harder on Reef's cock. Moving together, Reef rocked into him as Ford arched his back, pressing his ass hard into Reef's groin. Harder and faster, they moved until the slap of their bodies together – and the sloshing of the water below them – penetrated the quiet night as loudly as their moans and grunts. Their mating was wild, primitive. Ford's vision blacked out before it lit with a lightshow, more spectacular than the Aurora Borealis he'd seen on his visit to Sweden a few years earlier. Ribbons of cum shot from him, painting his chin and the decking around the Jacuzzi with its intensity. A strangled shout from behind him was the only other noise loud enough to match his own roar.

Slumping down, Ford was grateful for Reef as he supported Ford's boneless body, shudders still racking through them. Sucking in deep breaths, Ford floated in the post-orgasmic bliss cocooning him. There was only a moment to miss the stretching sensation of Reef's cock as it slipped from his depths, before Reef slid his fingers in and worked at Ford's sensitive prostate. It only took a few strokes and he was hard as nails once more and ready to explode. Reef wrapped his hand— still lubed up from their earlier round—around Ford's shaft, and pumped until his entire body stiffened again. Fire shot through him – spontaneous combustion. He bowed to Reef's masterful touch. Jet after jet of cum shot from Ford, emptying what little he had left in his balls into the bubbling water. Completely breathless, his throat hoarse from his shouts, Ford collapsed forward. Reef gathered him in his arms to keep his head above water. Sated, Ford closed his eyes and turned his face, nuzzling into the man who'd played his body like a finely tuned instrument and taken him to heights he'd never imagined before.

Silence enveloped them as they relaxed together, cuddling into one another's big bodies.

THE TWO WEEKS which passed since Reef moved his belongings into Ford's house were bliss. They'd christened every surface in and out of the cottage. Snowy days and nights had given them the excuse to stay in bed and map every inch of each other's bodies. Ford's favorite times were the sneaky touches and heated—and shy—glances. He grinned as he read the movie critic's review of the action flick they'd seen in town a few days earlier, after Reef had talked him into trying another coffee.

"*Come on, hon, let's see it. It'll be good.*"

"*You said that about the coffee. Then you fed me a girlie drink,*" Ford complained good naturedly.

"*It was the only way you'd drink it,*" Reef retorted, throwing his hands up in the air.

"*Whipped cream, though? Really?*" Ford playfully punched him in the arm.

"*You love whipped cream.*"

"*Oh my God, you didn't just say that.*" Ford laughed.

"*I'll make it worth your while.*" Reef grinned, wiggling his eyebrows, his gaze flicking down to the bulge that Ford perpetually had in his jeans when Reef was around.

"*Sure, why not? I'm always up for action.*"

"*You absolutely are.*" Reef laughed.

Reef dragged him to the back row of the theatre and picked two corner seats right up against the wall. There weren't many people in there – a clear Thursday morning after a big snow dump meant that most of the tourists were on the slopes and the locals were working. And that was absolutely fine with Ford. The opening scene had barely started when Reef was on him, pushing him down on the seat and straddling him. Reef's lips

connected with his and before they knew it, the lights to
the theatre were back on and the ushers were cleaning
up.

The color that stained Reef's cheeks when he sat up
made Ford laugh. "Come on, sweet cheeks. Let's go. I
need to get you naked." Ford held out his hand, but Reef
shook his head, looking at the usher closest to them. A
little hurt, Ford walked a step back as they left the
theatre.

———

THEY'D BEEN out in town again twice since then,
but there hadn't been any more PDA's yet; Reef pulled
back a little when they were out together. But that was
going to change.

"So, what should we do today?" Reef asked,
rubbing his eyes as he wandered into the kitchen
wearing nothing but his sleepy expression.

"I'm taking you out for the day," Ford said as he
wrapped his arms around Reef's body. Warm skin
against his palms had him humming as he brushed his
lips against his man's. Nuzzling into Reef's throat, Ford
kissed a line to his jaw.

"Do I get to know where?"

"Nope, it's a surprise," Ford murmured. The

Sunday markets were on in town. Live music, food stalls, artsie gifts, and people everywhere made for a good afternoon in the winter sunshine and Ford had every intention of showing Reef off to the masses.

"HMM, I LIKE THIS," Reef whispered as he pressed a kiss to the exposed skin at his throat. Dressed in faded jeans and a dark grey pullover, he'd been going for casual. But apparently with the way Reef was reacting, he'd pulled off sexy too. Looking over at Reef he was hard-pressed not to drool, his man looked damn fine. The grey cable knit sweater made Ford want to cuddle into him, to grab him around the waist and never let go. Well, that, and strip him out of it and shag him on the kitchen table.

They pulled on their boots, and after the quick ride into town, Ford drove into the parking lot. "So, where to?" Reef asked.

"To get some food and coffee in us and make you the number one son around."

"How am I achieving that?"

"You're buying something for Momma Bear and Coach from the markets we're headed to. She was pretty pissed that you wouldn't tell her anything about your new lady friend." Ford sent a sideways smirk to his boyfriend. Since Reef had been staying at his house, Ford heard him chatting on the phone with Momma Bear frequently. They had a great relationship and it warmed Ford's heart hearing the love that flowed between the two of them. Coach was a little harder to read, but the one thing that stood out in their conversations was how unconditionally proud of Reef Coach was.

"There was nothing to tell," Reef said innocently. "Now, if she'd asked me about the hot slab of muscle I'm sleeping with, I would have told her all about you."

"I know you're still scared of their reaction, but you know that I'm here for you no matter what, don't you? We'll deal with whatever happens together."

"Yeah, I know." Reef nodded and reached for Ford's hand. "I'm getting there. I'm hoping that they're okay with it. The thought of losing them still scares the shit outta me."

"I know I haven't been part of the conversations you've had and I don't know them like you do, but they love you. I have a good feeling about you telling them."

"Okay, soon."

As they rounded the corner, the markets came into view. Set along the lakeside park, the booths lined the sidewalk leaving a large open area where people milled around eating, talking and playing a game of rugby.

"That place has good coffee. Let's start there." Ford grinned, dragging Reef toward the nearby stand. The aroma of freshly ground beans filled his senses and Ford inhaled deeply. He'd never liked coffee until now. Reef's addiction was rubbing off on him. Not the taste, he still cringed at that – especially after Reef's effort a few days earlier - but the smell of the rich roast always transported Ford right back into that ranger's cabin during the whiteout, turning him on as he pictured Reef's naked body sliding into the tub for the first time. Reef ordered his coffee and Ford guided them over to the stone wall that ran the length of the marina. Sitting on the ledge, he pulled Reef into his arms, slipping one hand down the front of his sweater, humming at the heat of his skin through the tee underneath. Leaning in, Ford kissed his throat letting his tongue dance against Reef's sensitive, ticklish skin. Laughing, Reef tried to pull away but Ford held tight.

"Na-uh. You're mine, sweet cheeks."

Reef turned to him and smiled, those sexy dimples appearing with his wide grin, his warm brown eyes lighting up. "Always, honeybuns."

THEY WILED the rest of the morning away, meandering through the myriad of stands together. Ford had no idea of the sort of present he'd buy for his parents if he were looking for them at the markets. He came from old money. His mother expected jewelry from her favorite designer. There was no way she would be seen wearing the broach that Reef picked out for Momma Bear. Handmade from New Zealand jade and freshwater pearls, the design was simple, beautiful and when Reef saw it, his face lit up in one of those smiles that sent Ford's heart stuttering.

When Reef did the same thing with the set of freshwater flies and lures, Ford almost laughed at the thought of his own father fishing. Stratford Senior was simply too sophisticated for that.

"Come on, let's go listen to the band." Ford motioned to the musicians setting up their electric acoustic guitars on the small makeshift stage. They sat down on the grass just as the guitarists started playing an old bluegrass song.

Reef got a couple of hotdogs loaded with all the trimmings and two plastic cups filled with beer. Ford looked at the mass of onion, ketchup, mustard, bun and sausage, and raised his eyebrow at Reef. "You eat it. Like this," Reef said, grinning at him before taking a massive bite out of the food, devouring half of it in two bites.

"I usually eat my sausage a little differently."

"Oh, I bet." Reef laughed.

"I was talking about bangers and mash. Get your mind out of the gutter," Ford chided him playfully.

"But it's so much fun there." Ford laughed at Reef's pout and hauled him down to the ground, climbing on top and kissing him. Reef soon let go of the hotdog and reached for Ford's hair, spearing his fingers through the curls and holding Ford in place while their tongues tangled. The taste of hot dog and beer in their kiss had Ford wanting more, delving in deeper, taking and giving into the playful tug of war they were swept away in.

Pulling back, Ford rested his forehead against Reef's. "I want you too much. I won't be able to stop if we keep going and last time I checked, showing my lily white ass in public while I shag you, would get me arrested."

Reef chuckled. "As much as I love your lily white ass, I'd rather not spend the night in the lock up."

"Come to think of it though, jail sex could be fun. Hands cuffed behind your back, bent over while I strip search you," Ford murmured as he nibbled Reef's throat.

"Except that it'd probably be some old, balding cop with a beer belly and a hairy back doing the strip searching." Ford kept kissing him as he tweaked Reef's nipple through his pullover making him buck his hips, grinding against Ford.

"Like fuck. No chance in hell another man is touching you."

"Are you a little jealous, hon?"

"No, just tellin' you that no Bobby's gonna get frisky with his night stick with you."

"I fuckin' love your accent, Ford. Say 'you're nicked' for me."

"You're nicked, sweet cheeks. You have the right to remain silent, but anything you do say turns me on—"

IT WAS one of the best days Reef had had in years. They'd walked and talked, laughed and listened to a few great musicians, relaxing on the grassy knoll laying in each other's arms. Reef was sure he'd fallen asleep at one stage, his head resting on Ford's shoulder as he'd enjoyed Ford's strong fingers massaging his back. It was how they slept most nights. Even in sleep, Ford's protective instinct dominated him, always pulling Reef into his arms. That was fine with Reef too. Who'd have thought that a muscular chest would have been the most comfortable pillow he'd ever had? They were both warm bodies, so sleeping naked was the norm, especially when they used the down comforter too. That had paved the way for more bed-time, middle-of-the-night and morning sessions than he'd ever had before. They say that gay men have more sex than hetero couples – Reef had no doubt that was true if he and Ford were anything like typical bisexual men. *Now that's weird, thinking of myself as bisexual.*

"HERE'S YOUR BEER." Ford handed him the bottle as he sat down next to Reef in the booth at the sports bar they'd walked into. The sun had dropped below the ridgeline earlier that evening and a chill permeated the air. Instead of heading back to the house, Ford suggested they eat out again and led them down an alley, up a set of rickety stairs and through a beat up door to a bar with atmosphere like no other. Ford hadn't reached for his hand when they'd arrived, so Reef hadn't pushed. He didn't exactly want to be a secret, but he wasn't going to ruin things by going all diva on his boyfriend, especially when Ford's friends invited the two of them to join them. The guy named Trent had sneered at him when they'd been re-introduced. He was one of the rescuers that had picked them up from the ranger's cabin, but as usual Reef had forgotten his name.

Instead of shaking his hand as Ford's other friends, Ricky – the helicopter pilot who'd helped Ford - and Angelo, his brother, had done, that dude upped and left. Reef was all for a live and let live attitude but if looks could kill, the guy would have stabbed both their eyes out. Reef was glad that he hadn't stuck around. Trent would have been a serious buzz kill to his mojo.

"Burgers are on their way," Reef replied, placing a coaster in front of Ford. He sat back watching how Ford interacted with his friends, careful not to stare at his sex-on-a-stick boyfriend. He was probably failing but he didn't want to out Ford. It was up to him when, or even if, he told his friends. Being out among strangers was different, but here with friends? He understood Ford's hesitancy. For Reef, keeping the secret was easier because of the distance between him and the only people that mattered. Still, the stress of speaking with Momma Bear and Coach was starting to weigh on him. Reef knew he had to tell them soon. Even though it was new, he and Ford were too serious to pretend they were just a fling anymore. The two of them had spent nearly every waking moment together over the last few weeks. He'd fallen hard. Ford's charm, his flirting, his sweet gestures and possessive side all had Reef's heart doing flip-flops.

"When are you going back to work, Ford?" Ricky asked.

"Next week. Knee's pretty much all healed up."

"Good, man. That's great news." Ricky held out his bottle of beer, and they clinked the necks together.

"Okay, give us the low down. How were the sponge baths, Ford?" Angelo asked. Turning toward Reef, Angelo explained, "This bastard scores all the girls. Bats his eyes and flashes a smile, and they fall over themselves to go home with him."

"Ang." Ford warned.

"What's the bet Ricky? Two, three numbers?"

"What the fuck is it with people asking me that question?" Ford threw his hands up in the air.

Ricky looked closely at Reef, smiling slightly as he did. Reef didn't turn his gaze away, didn't blink. Instinctively, he knew this was one of those tests of character, not a pissing match for dominance, just a silent battle to prove to Ford's friend that Reef was worthy of Ford's time.

"Nah, man, no girls," Ricky murmured. There was no teasing tone in his voice, no ridicule. Just a straight out statement of the facts.

"So, lads, I... ah..." Ford started, then hesitated. Grasping Reef's hand under the table, he took a deep breath and began again. "Reef and I are together."

Ricky broke out in a grin, slapping Ford's shoulder and congratulating him. "I knew there was something between you. Plain as day when I saw you at the cabin."

"Nah, not then. You finding us in the tub was completely innocent. Well, kind of."

"You might not have been together or done anything, but even a blind man could have seen the connection between the two of you."

Reef couldn't help but smile at that. Ricky was a good guy.

"Ang?" Ford asked.

"Together? Like boyfriends?"

"Like boyfriends, yes," Ford added, lifting their interlinked hands to the top of the table.

"Aren't you straight?" Angelo blurted out.

"Apparently not as straight as I thought. Listen, I don't want to be a prick, but if you've got a problem with us—"

"No, not at all, dude. I'm kinda shocked. I didn't expect that. Last time I saw you, you had a girl hanging off you."

"People change. I've changed." Ford smiled at Reef, his gaze full of affection as he squeezed Reef's hand.

"Good for you, Ford. I'm happy for the two of you.

Love is love and all that shit. And good sex is even better." Angelo raised his bottle.

"I'll toast to that," Reef added joining the conversation for the first time and grinning at Ford. Ford didn't hesitate, raising his bottle in the air as he leaned in and pressed his lips to Reef's.

Until that moment Reef had felt the need to hold a piece of himself back. But knowing that Ford wouldn't hesitate to stand up for him, for them, comforted Reef. He knew he had a goofy grin plastered all over his face, but he didn't care. He was happy. For the first time in his life, he was... complete.

AS THEIR WAITRESS collected the empty plates from the table, 'Uptown Funk' started blaring through the speakers. Ford grinned and squeezed Reef's hand. "Come on, sweet. Let's dance."

"I don't dance, Ford. I'm not drunk enough for that."

"You do now, and you are." Ford laughed, tugging on his arm, like a little kid in a candy store. He pulled Reef up, saying, "And you won't need this," as he lifted Reef's sweater over his head before doing the same to his and dropping them on the chairs they'd been sitting in. They stepped toward the dance floor that had started to fill up with the song and Ford pulled him into his arms, pressing a leg between his. Moving slowly, Ford was completely out of sync with the fast beat. Laughing, Reef joined in, wrapping his arms around his man. It started out light-hearted, but the song soon morphed into another, a remix of the Charlie Puth's 'One Call Away.' As the heavy beat enveloped them, the world around Reef faded away and their bodies moved together in a sensuous grind. Staring into each other's eyes, desire and need flamed between them. Reef's fingers found their way into Ford's hair, pulling him closer. Ford's warm breath ghosted over his cheek as they moved. Ford's tight grip around his waist had Reef spinning, lost in the music, lost in his man. They could have been the only two people in the bar, hell the universe, and Reef wouldn't have noticed. Ford's hands under his tee, kneading the muscle at the base of Reef's spine felt like heaven. They gravitated toward each other, barely a hair's breadth between them. Eyes drifting closed, their mouths joined and their bodies swayed, moving to the sexual rhythm they now knew so well. Reef hummed as Ford's tongue slipped past his lips. The taste of beer and lemon meringue pie – which Ford had eaten for dessert – filled his senses. Running one hand down Ford's back, Reef pulled him closer, deepening their kiss, giving himself over to Ford completely.

"Dude, we're out," snapped Reef out of the bubble he was in with Ford. It was Ricky.

"Okay, lads. See you soon," Ford responded. Angelo looked completely flustered, licking his lips before he nodded and made a hasty exit. Reef was pulled in for another kiss with a smile, Ford not waiting for anyone else to speak. And that was fine by Reef. Laughing, their lips joined as they moved once more to the music.

"WANT SOME AIR?" Reef asked as they each chugged a bottle of water at the bar.

"Mmhmm."

Tugging their discarded pullovers on, they stepped out into the cold night air. "Come on, let's take a walk down by the lake. It's on the way to my truck." Ford motioned, pointing to the rocky waterfront.

Reef stood by the water's edge looking out over the still surface, hands in his pockets. Ford's actions tonight had flipped a switch in him. Coming out to his friends couldn't have been easy. Reef could see the tension vibrating off Ford when he'd tried to say it the first time, needing his strength to be able to say the words.

Seeing Ford's bravery gave him the balls to tell Momma Bear and Coach too. The easiest way to do it would be over Skype, but easy wasn't necessarily right. He needed to see their reactions in person, needed to be able to stop them if they tried to walk away. He only had one option - do it face to face. They were flying out to see him in a month during his pre-season training in Calgary. Could he wait that long? He didn't really have any other choice. The only downside was that Ford wouldn't be there. It'd be months between when Reef left and he and Ford could see each other again. That knowledge put a dampener on Reef's spirit. How were they going to be apart for so long without going stir-crazy? Long distance relationships had never worked for him. He'd always gone with the flow, never overly worried about making it work. But now? The thought of losing Ford because of miles separating them made Reef rethink his career, his entire lifestyle.

"Hey you okay, sweet cheeks?" Ford asked as he nudged Reef's elbow with his own.

"God, that's the corniest pet name. Why'd we stick with them?"

"You can't pick your pet name. It's earned, given to you." Ford motioned to the large boulders next to them. "Let's sit."

"You're thinking of astronauts, not couples, dumbass. Don't you watch *Big Bang?*" Reef grinned, elbowing Ford playfully.

"Where'd you go? You were off with the fairies."

"Was thinking about my pre-season training. We're not gonna be together for a while. I'm gonna miss you."

"Actually, about that, you know how I'm supposed to go back to work next week?"

"Yeah," Reef replied, nodding.

"I might have overstepped the boundary a little. If I did, it's okay, I don't have to do it."

"Do what, Ford?"

"Come with you to Calgary." Ford held up his hand, motioning as if to stop Reef from speaking but Reef was too shocked to say anything. Here he pictured being separated from Ford for most of the next seven or eight months, but if Ford could go to Canada too, they'd be able to spend the eight weeks of his pre-season training together. Could it be any better?

"I spoke with the director of the resort you're training at. She and I have known each other for a few years and, anyway, I called in a favor. She can fit me into their roster on the slopes. I probably won't be doing rescues, but they have an opening – one of their ski instructors got injured and another found out she's pregnant and doesn't want to be outside in the cold anymore. I'd need to give a couple of weeks notice before finishing up here so they can redo the rosters, but I'll be able to get there about three weeks after you do." Ford stopped talking and looked down, no longer meeting Reef's gaze. Reef sat up straighter and turned to him, still trying to put his shock and excitement into words.

"I'm sorry, never mind. It was stupid of me to—"

"Shut up, Ford." Reef lifted his face with a finger under his chin, brushing his thumb over his bottom lip. "You'd do that for me? For us? So we could be together?"

"Yeah." He nodded. "I want to be with you, but I didn't want to suggest anything unless I could get work over there. It's hard to manage the mortgage repayments if I take much more time off than the regular seasons."

Reef didn't hesitate, he climbed on top of Ford, straddling him. Cupping his face, Reef brushed his lips gently over Ford's.

"If you leave early, can you still come back to Queenstown next season? You won't be burning your bridges here, will you?"

"I can come back. My director's a romantic. He understood when I spoke with him about it. You're killing me, Reef. Do you want me to come?"

"Hell yeah," Reef murmured before pressing their mouths together, taking Ford in a scorching kiss. Tongues and teeth clashing, it was full of fire, full of need. They only broke apart to take in a lungful of much needed oxygen. Resting his forehead against Ford's, Reef ran his fingers through the curls at the nape of Ford's neck.

"You think I could come and train here during my off-season?"

"I'll dig out the bowl with a fucking spoon if it means you being with me."

"And you'll hold my place while I'm gone?" Reef asked, gazing into the bluest of blue eyes.

"Me and you? Us? We're permanent. I'll always wait for you, always be faithful. I'll always hold your spot."

"This is one of those times that you need to kiss me again, Ford."

"My pleasure, sweet cheeks." And he did exactly that, stealing Reef's breath once more.

Making love to his mouth.

Sealing their promise.

Connecting them together.

THE END... FOR NOW

WHITE NOISE

UNEXPECTED BOOK TWO

Reef and Ford's story continues...

Steam floated out of the open bathroom door, as Ford stepped in the doorway listening to Reef hum. He'd recognize that sound anywhere — Reef was content, happy. And so was Ford. He watched the soapy water cascade down his lover's body. Arms resting against the tiled walls, Reef's head dropped low, Ford admired the view. His muscled back, tight ass, and lean legs tempted Ford to strip and join him. It wasn't exactly a hardship to do that either. Ford tugged off his black

Henley, and stepped toward the shower just as Reef dropped his hand, and shut off the faucet, shaking his hair out. Ordinarily he'd be disappointed, but Ford just wanted to be close to him, to touch him and rediscover every inch of this man's body.

He picked up the fluffy white towel from the nearby hook and held it out ready to wrap around Reef. "Come on out here, sweet cheeks. Let me look after you."

"Mmm, you spoil me," he murmured as he stepped into Ford's embrace, Reef's back to his front. Reef tilted his head back, resting it in the crook of Ford's neck, the wet strands of his blond hair tickling Ford's bare shoulder. Breathing deep, he inhaled the fresh clean scent of Reef's shampoo: the outdoors and that essence which was uniquely Reef. Together, it was Ford's favorite smell.

"No more than you deserve." Ford ran the towel down Reef's shoulders and arms. Rubbing down his back, Ford dropped a kiss on the pale skin as he moved around to Reef's front. He gently dried Reef's hair, massaging his scalp through the material. Tugging it off, he moved the towel over Reef's chest. This was what he needed; to be caring for his man. A warm glow blazed through his chest, right over his heart.

As he swiped the towel gently over Reef's skin,

Ford followed his path with kisses, reacquainting himself with every muscle and plane of Reef's body. Dropping to his knees, Ford dried Reef's legs and feet, before kissing each of his muscled thighs, the soft hairs tickling his lips. He struggled to resist the temptation to bury his face into Reef's groin and run his mouth over every inch of him. Instead, he stood, and with Reef's hand in his, guided them toward the bed.

Reef nuzzled into him as Ford wrapped his arms around his man, drawing Reef into his embrace. They laid like that, Reef's head on his chest, their legs wound around each other as Ford breathed in the smell of comfort and home. God he was so happy, it was sickening.

"Wanna tell me why your mother's ringtone is from the *Wizard of Oz*?" Reef asked quietly.

"Cause she's pretty much the Wicked Witch?"

"You're gonna tell your parents about us?" Reef asked dropping a kiss on his pec as he tickled Ford's oblique with barely-there touches of his fingertips.

"Yeah. I asked her to book some flights over. She and Father are arriving week after next."

"Cool." Reef's tone spoke volumes, and contrary to what he said, he wasn't cool about it.

"Is it?"

Reef propped himself up on his elbows and looked

down at him, breaking their head to toe connection. "You don't have to tell them, Ford."

"I want to. But is it cool with you? You sound nervous."

Reef looked at him through wide, surprised eyes. "Are you serious? Of course I'm freaking out about it." He held out his fist, counting on his fingers as he spoke. "I'm meeting one of the most highly respected surgeons in London, he's ridiculously smart and has such high expectations for you. Even if I managed to somehow satisfy every other one of their demands in a partner for you, I'd fail the most important one; I'm a man for fuck sake. That isn't gonna make 'em happy, Ford. Yeah, I'm nervous."

———

Smoothing down his scarf and wiping his sweaty palms on his jeans, Ford took a hold of his wrist. "Sweet, calm down. It's gonna be okay."

"I can't. I'm freakin' out." Fidgeting, Reef shifted in his seat. Anxiety raced through his system. He'd never once been this tense — not even in a competition — never been so adrift in his life. Heart racing and unable to take anything but short, sharp breaths, Reef's vision started swimming. Ford's finger on his wrist disappeared, replaced with a hand at the nape of his neck, pushing his head down to his knees.

"Long slow breaths, Reef. I've gotcha, you're okay." All Reef's focus zeroed in on the warm palm anchoring him to Ford. The dizziness cleared as his heart rate and breathing slowed to their normal pace. He mustered every technique yoga had taught him and closed his eyes imagining himself at the top of a peak, the cold wind fanning his face. Thinking about the mountains, the serenity surrounding him when that blanket of white stretched before him, his zen returned and Reef sat up. "You okay?" Ford asked, his hand back on his wrist now monitoring his slowing heartbeat.

"Yeah, think so." Reef looked away, embarrassed.

"Hey, Reef, look at me," Ford implored. Reef took a deep breath and turned in his seat ashamed he couldn't handle the stress. Ford had also unbuckled his belt and was facing him. Taking his face in his palms, Ford pulled him forward so their foreheads pressed together. "Whatever happens in there, we're together. This doesn't change us, it doesn't matter. It's a courtesy to my parents, that's all. I want you; no one else. They may not be happy about us, but it doesn't matter. I don't care about their opinion, I care about you."

Reef held onto Ford's waist like a lifeline. Grounding him, his man smiled, and Reef couldn't have turned away even if he'd wanted to. Ford brushed his lips whisper-soft against Reef's and he melted into the touch. "Kinda nerve-racking meeting them, that's all. I don't want to create a bad impression. I want to be good enough for you."

"You are, sweet. No matter what gets said in there, no matter what happens you and I walk out together. We're solid. Yeah?"

"Yeah." Reef nodded, smiling for the first time since they'd left the townhouse.

"Pinkie-swear?" Ford held out his pinkie to Reef, the rest of his hand in a fist, eyebrows raised and a wicked grin curving his lips. Reef snorted out a laugh, before curling his own pinkie around Ford's.

"Pinkie-swear it." Turning to look toward the not-so-imposing front door and thinking about the frigid reception he knew he was going to get still made his balls shrivel up. "Let's get this over with."

"That's the spirit. Exactly my thoughts whenever I see the doctor and his wife." Ford leaned in and kissed Reef with a hard press of his lips before pulling away and throwing open the door of the SUV. Reef mirrored his actions and met Ford at the bottom of the stone staircase. With Ford's hand pressed against the small of his back, Reef let him guide them to the door. Before pressing the buzzer,

Ford turned to him and smiled, leaning in for a slow kiss.

"Hello Stratford, please do come in." A lady, who Reef guessed was Ford's mother, motioned for them to enter the chalet. Her perfectly coiffed blonde bob barely moved as she stepped back out of the cold Canadian wind. Dressed in a white calf-length skirt, a pale pink cashmere sweater, and white pumps, she radiated old money. She instantly reminded Reef of the Queen of England. Maybe it was just the accent, or perhaps it was the way she carried herself. The diamond jewelry she wore — which rivaled the royal crown in cut and clarity — didn't hurt either.

"Mother, how are you?" Ford kissed her on the cheek, before stepping over the threshold and unbuttoning his heavy woolen coat, and removing his scarf.

When her gaze momentarily flicked to Reef, it was enough for him to see the surprise in her pale blue eyes, but it quickly disappeared. Unmoving after Ford greeted her, she held her head high as she spoke, her tone filled with an air of superiority and primness Reef had never experienced before. "Well thank you, Stratford. And you?"

"Stellar." Ford cracked a grin at Reef, warming his heart and easing the tension knotting his muscles.

A little.

Maybe.

Hell, who was he kidding, Reef was a wreck, even more so now he'd seen what Ford's mother looked like. This meeting the parents' thing? Fucking awful.

As they stood in the large foyer taking off the heavy outer layer of clothes, Ford's father entered. There was no mistaking the two were related. If Reef wanted to know what his man would look like in thirty years, all he had to do was check out his father. They had the same bright blue eyes, but where Ford's blues sparked with life, and were full of mischievous fun, his father's were cold. Shrewd. Gray hair cropped close to his head, and disguising the wave contrasted with Ford's chocolate brown curls, curls Reef could barely get enough of. Ford was sure to develop laugh lines near his eyes and around his groomed stubble. His father's face was unmarked in those spots. Instead, he had a concentration frown currently marring his otherwise smooth face.

"Stratford." Ford's father nodded at Reef's man, and shook his hand. What sort of father does that? Seriously, a handshake? They hadn't seen each other for months. Sure, they'd made the trip to Canada at Ford's request, but still. As he observed them, Reef could see evidence of the quirks Ford had mentioned when speaking of his parents. They shook hands like business associates, a healthy distance between them and without any hint of a smile. They presented a united front; Ford's mother stood by her husband's side, equally stiff, her hands clasped together in front of her body. While Ford's father ignored Reef entirely, his mother made no effort to hide the disdain in her gaze directed exclusively at Reef. Ford may have a strained relationship with his parents, but even Reef expected more happiness in their greeting. What Ford was putting up with was ridiculous. When he'd seen Momma Bear and Coach, he'd been wrapped in hugs all round, his face peppered with kisses from his flamboyant 'adopted' mom. Even his real parents, whom he barely spoke to, showed Reef more affection than Ford's were at that moment.

"Mother, Father, may I present Reef Reid, my boyfriend."

ABOUT THE AUTHOR

By day Ann Grech lives in the corporate world and can be found sitting behind a desk typing away at reports and papers or lecturing to a room full of students. She graduated with a PhD in 2016 and is now an over-qualified nerd. Glasses, briefcase, high heels and a pencil skirt, she's got the librarian look nailed too. If only they knew! She swears like a sailor, so that's got to be a hint. The other one was "the look" from her tattoo artist when she told him that she wanted her kids initials "B" and "J" tattooed on her foot. It took a second to register that it might be a bad idea.

She's never entirely fit in and loves escaping into a book—whether it's reading or writing one. But she's found her tribe now and loves her MM book world family. She dislikes cooking, but loves eating, can't figure out technology, but is addicted to it, and her guilty pleasure is Byron Bay Cookies. Oh and shoes. And lingerie. And maybe handbags too. Well, if we're being honest, we'd probably have to add her library too given the state of her credit card every month (what can she say, she's a bookworm at heart)!

She also publishes her raunchier short stories under her pen name, Olive Hiscock.

Ann loves chatting to people online, so if you'd like to keep up with what she's got going on:

Join her newsletter:
http://anngrech.us8.list-manage2.com/subscribe?u=oaf7475c0791ed8f1466e7fd9&id=1cee9cdcb6

Like her on Facebook:
https://www.facebook.com/pages/Ann-Grech/458420227655212

Join her reader group:
https://www.facebook.com/groups/1871698189780535/

Follow her on Twitter:
@anngrechauthor

Follow her on Goodreads:
https://www.goodreads.com/author/show/7536397.Ann_Grech

Follow her on BookBub:
https://www.bookbub.com/authors/ann-grech

Follow her on Instagram: @anngrechauthor

Visit her website for her current booklist:
www.anngrech.com

She'd love to hear from you directly, too. Please feel free to e-mail her at ann@anngrech.com or check out her website www.anngrech.com for updates.

 twitter.com/anngrechauthor

instagram.com/anngrechauthor

www.ingramcontent.com/pod-product-compliance
Lightning Source LLC
Chambersburg PA
CBHW031244120726
47905CB00002B/718